LOVEENOUGH

ALSO BY DIONNE BRAND

FICTION

In Another Place, Not Here
At the Full and Change of the Moon
What We All Long For
Sans Souci and Other Stories

POETRY

'Fore Day Morning
Earth Magic
Winter Epigrams and Epigrams to Ernesto Cardenal in Defense of Claudia
Primitive Offensive
Chronicles of the Hostile Sun
No Language Is Neutral
Land to Light On
thirsty
Inventory
Ossuaries
Chronicles: Early Works

NON-FICTION

Bread Out of Stone
No Burden to Carry
A Map to the Door of No Return

LOVE
ENOUGH

DIONNE BRAND

ALFRED A. KNOPF CANADA

PUBLISHED BY ALFRED A. KNOPF CANADA

Copyright © 2014 Dionne Brand

www.randomhouse.ca

Knopf Canada and colophon are registered trademarks.

Library and Archives Canada Cataloguing in Publication

Brand, Dionne, author
Love enough : a novel / Dionne Brand.

Issued in print and electronic formats.

ISBN 978-0-345-80888-2
eBook ISBN 978-0-345-80890-5

I. Title.

PS8553.R275L69 2014   C813'.54   C2014-902437-1

Text and cover design by Terri Nimmo
Cover images: detail from Caza con reclamo by
Francisco de Goya © Museo Nacional del Prado, Madrid;
(butterfly) © Carlosphotos / Dreamstime.com

Printed and bound in the United States of America

2 4 6 8 9 7 5 3 1

LOVEENOUGH

ONE

The best way of looking at a summer sunset in this city
is in the rear-view mirror. Or better, the side mirrors
of a car. So startling. All the subtlety, the outerworldliness
of the sunset follows you. If only you could drive that way
forever. It's counterintuitive, you understand, but you get a
wide measure of that quotidian beauty. If you ever travel
east along Dupont Street, at that time, look back. Despite
this not being a particularly handsome street—in fact it is
most often grim—you may see, looking back, looking
west, something breathtaking. It is perhaps because this
street is so ugly; car-wrecking shops, taxi dispatch sheds,

rooming houses, hardware stores, desolate all-night diners
and front yards eaten up by a hundred winters' salt; it is
because of all this that a sunset is in the perfect location
here. Needed.

And later you can see moons here too, rounding perfectly
over a derelict building where artists and musicians live.
Or vagrant, over the personal storage depot filled with
rooms of regret—unpaid for and best forgotten. Then too,
undressed, over the abandoned fish store, and flaring, over
the wheel alignment garage.

June. She lives only two streets away. On Salem. She
could walk. But she drives along here, on Dupont Street,
in the evenings just to be taken up by a glimpse of beauty
in that rear-view mirror. You might ask, beauty? Yes, she
would say, beauty. She is not the type who is happy the
way other people are happy.

The other day, June and Sydney were out running along
the waterfront trail. Lake Ontario, barely recovered from
toxic effluent, was a salvaging green. The sky was violet; a
violet soft with polymers and hydrocarbons, and June saw
two small blue butterflies mating near the lake. It was just
beside the dogwood bushes. Summer Azures. She stopped.
Her heart felt feathery at the sight. She was on the verge of

crying when Sydney said, "Only people like you notice that kind of thing."

"People like me?"

"Hm hm, people who watch everything all the time."

June heard a splashing of water, it ripped right across her heart. It might have been a duck on the lake or a swan. She saw a half moon drizzled in violet polysulfides. She saw the east side of the city dissolving across the lake.

"Who do you think you are anyway, Sydney?" A small rage overtook her at this notion that all she did was watch. "I have done so many things you will never, never understand."

"Like what?" Sydney didn't mean to say that, but small rages were infectious with them.

A bird flew by, black, with red underwings. A gaunt man in a coat, a woman with red hair were ahead of them on the boardwalk.

"Just because you cannot make out two butterflies ... fucking, is no reason to insult me."

The lilac sky was greying out. More synthetic than sky. The nuclear plant to the east had been altering the clouds by degrees for decades. "Insult? My god, I'm glad you can see two butterflies fucking. That's all I was trying to say!"

"Now they're gone." June was blue too.

The gaunt man in the coat, the woman with the red hair were ahead of them still, closer now. The woman bent down, as if crouching, the man waved an arm like an axe above her. A gull lifted off the lake. June took off, ran past them, leaving Sydney behind. She made her way to the locks and behind the sandbanks, disappearing from Sydney's view. She felt like running to Hamilton, sixty-six kilometres away; they say you can do that running along this path. But it's not Hamilton that June wants to go to.

She wants to get out of her own head, a stoop from which she can pick a fight with the most benevolent human being in the world. Even when the sky is lilac or violet and even if two butterflies stop her day with their urgent life, she hovers on this stoop like a praying mantis, looking harmless but not at all harmless. Her stick of a body is deceptive. Her poised look, her brain in compressed rage—all the reedy details of a life lived cautiously and suspiciously yet on the verge of weeping at small beautiful occurrences.

Sydney catches up to June and runs beside her silently towards Hamilton. They run now in a coming twilight. Glass condominiums ride their right shoulders to the end of the waterfront path. To their left the lake meets the Humber River. They are just trying to run out June's anger and unreasonableness and Sydney's failure to be quiet and observe.

Silence is how they make peace. Usually each works out the facts and fictions in her own mind, the way one does, forgetting one's own part and then forgetting the other's part. Finally each won't remember the whole fight clearly and they'll leave it at that. The dregs of a fight, though, can be more dangerous than the fight itself, since these dregs are a synthesis of collective arguments over time. A concentrated toxin. No argument in the world is ever resolved. Resolving would suggest some liquid in which arguments could be immersed, perhaps love. But it must be love enough. The consistency of the mixture would have to be a greater portion of love. So many decilitres of love to dissolve so many millilitres of the other stuff. And the trouble is, this "other stuff," this toxic material, is sometimes flammable. These other ingredients are random and personal, like childhood or desire and they don't necessarily mix well with love. Love is not as durable or pliable as one is led to think anyway. Love can be indefinable all on its own. But this fight, the one about the butterflies, will be remembered with humour eventually because after all it was only about two butterflies mating, not the greater matters of the world.

June was in love once. Truly. She sometimes comes upon the memory in the form of a breathless panic. Then she closes that door quickly. It took place in a bachelor apartment, and at the Yonge subway station, and during several springs. She was twenty.

At the Yonge subway station. She remembers waiting there on the southbound platform for the lover. Each train that came through the tunnel from where her lover lived ran up June's spine like a corkscrew. Late, always late, the lover would emerge like a gift, bright and innocent. As if not late at all, but on time. They would go to whatever movie or party or club in a radiant cylinder of what June now calls panic but then she called love. They would dance among other people in love too, encased in their own cylinders. These cylinders weren't smooth but jagged and electric to the touch, and, on the dance floor, June and the lover were a dangerous energy. They were exhausted and frantic in their desire, and all the other desires around them made them clash and incinerate. June heard a constant clanging in her ears. Her breath was like small sharp silver bracelets. When they parted at the Yonge subway station again, June felt suicidal and could not look down at the empty station rails.

The bachelor apartment where her lover lived was full of jasper rocks and sunlight no matter the weather outside. June spent days walking over the rocks and turning her face to the sunlight. She lost her part-time jobs at the daycare centre and at the Mac's Milk store where she stacked shelves because she spent so much time with the lover coupled on the rocks. The rocks were blood warm and June found red lichen on the lover's ankle.

Love lasted only one year but the time felt like several springs strung together. The lover said it was over long before June heard. When June did hear, her chest caved in and she put her hand there to stop it. The love was in pieces and June collected them and smoothed them over with her thumbs like you would a bird's wing or an envelope. After, she could not recall the lover's face, nor revisit the jagged ice and the coarse paper of their quarrels. June walked out of the apartment with its jasper and sunlight and up to now has not gone back to that street. She doesn't avoid that part of town, you wouldn't say that, but it is as if that street doesn't exist. It has been cut out of the street map of the city. The city limns there. Once or twice she saw the lover but it wasn't the same person. That made her wonder if we ever see people truly or if in fact, in love, we are simply teetering on that thin filament in the brain between the insula and the striatum. Alone. We are peering over a precipice in a particular quadrant of grey matter, frightening ourselves with a leap we cannot make. As we all do, June had expected her own reflection in the lover's face. Her reflection being a benign understanding. But the lover's face, in the end, was fierce and foreign. It wasn't the same person. Not someone June knew at all.

June doesn't visit that area in her mind anymore. That abyss is off limits unless something surprises her and she feels that panic again. A song or a door slamming is all it takes at times. And certainly the southbound train at Yonge subway station. So for years June never took this train, especially in the evenings, until they renovated the station and then it was a different place altogether.

TWO

Turning across Highway 7 to Brougham, the Beemer was ahead. The Audi followed, losing and finding the tail lights of the Beemer screwdriving along the highway. The road was unlit and Bedri conjured trees. Sweat poured into his eyes and he fought to stay in the glow of Ghost's tail lights. The road wound its way around Locust Hill then jogged east. He wondered if Ghost knew where he was going. He wondered, but he did not stop or press the car horn. The Beemer danced ahead in the now full darkness. He crouched over, gripping the steering, licking the sweat pouring down his face. The Beemer and the Audi

emerged out of forest and retreated into forest for half an
hour and then they came to a big crossing. Ghost made a
right turn and Bedri followed. They seemed to be driving
in squares. The line down the centre of the highway
glowed phosphorescent. It blinded Bedri in the left eye. He
didn't know if he was sweating or crying. He realised
they'd turned around and were heading back the way they'd
come. He leaned on the horn. He saw Ghost signal right
and followed him off the shoulder into a narrow driveway.
They drove down into a park, he saw a sign or half of the
sign, "Milne Conservation" it read. He slowed, stopped
and jumped out of the Audi, waving his hands in the dark
shouting, "Ghost! Ghost!" Ghost continued driving then
stopped about one hundred metres ahead.

Bedri ran toward the Beemer. Breathless when he arrived,
he said, "What the fuck, man?"

"Let's go," Ghost said, jumping out and spinning him
around. "Go! We're ditching it."

"Why?"

"Why? Shit, Money, you could never think. They'll be
on us quicker now."

"Then what did we do that for? Let's take it to the guy
in the east. The Audi ride too."

"He won't want this one now."

"Turn it off!" Bedri said. Ghost had left the car running.

"What?"

"Turn it off—someone will hear it."

"It's a fucking park, Money!"

"Turn it off! Fuck!"

Ghost reached into the car and turned the engine off. Then he angled sideways like a pitcher and threw the keys into the darkness. Bedri began to run back toward the Audi. Ghost dropped in beside him and they sprinted together.

Bedri had a thick body. Ever since he was a child he'd had difficulty running. He was running now though and his body didn't feel thick, it felt wet, steaming. It felt fleet. They couldn't keep the fucking car now; they beat a man to death. Maybe. And now they couldn't keep his fucking Beemer.

The hundred metres felt longer that it was. He couldn't feel his feet. Instead he felt like a fish swimming. Swimming beside Ghost. They got to the Audi and Bedri jumped into the driver's seat. His hands felt big. Ghost seemed like a hot pinpoint of fire beside him. Bedri's hands felt huge. They burned when he touched the steering wheel. They burned when he turned the key in the ignition. The key was hot as melting silver.

DIONNE BRAND

Ghost, his face lit, his body coiled, wiry, he was glad he didn't have to drive, his long fingers trembled, he felt like going to the bathroom, his body let off an odour, like iron. He wanted to say something wise or something cruel again but he was quiet.

Bedri drove. He drove fast. Something told him to drive slow, and he tried but he couldn't. He heard a yelp, it was coming from inside his head and it was coming out of his mouth but he clamped his lips shut holding it in. From the passenger seat he heard, "Whoa, whoa, man!" He lifted his foot off the gas. He should slow down.

"Whoa, man, you feel me? You feel me, Money? That was the bomb!" Ghost had found something to say and his mouth was saying it. *The bomb, the bomb.* Bedri tried to make sense of the word. He felt as if he had inhaled water, or coke, or air freshener. His nose was clear, a burning skittered over his forehead, under the bone near his eyes.

"Did you see that guy? Man, he was a mess. The guy was a mess."

Yes, Bedri had seen the face, the eyes swollen so quickly after one blow, it seemed. Yes, he saw the face. Fuck.

"We are thugged out, man! Thugged out!" Ghost's mouth found the exact words. Bedri felt Ghost's hand on his shoulder, brotherly and loving, it made him yell too.

"Yeah, yeah, thugged out." He heard his own voice turn to a croak, "The guy was messed up!" His croaking made no sense to him and his laughter made no sense to him. He was hardly looking at the road, his big swelling hands seemed to block out half the windscreen.

"Yeah, damn, Money. Damn!" Ghost's voice filled the car and Bedri felt it boom in his head.

Bedri yelled back, "Yeah, damn, Money, whoa! Fucker didn't want to give it up. Fucker, man!"

The noise in the car was overwhelming. They were both screaming and a hot mist from their bodies clouded the windscreen. Bedri lowered the driver's window. A cold shock of air came into the car though it was summer. A warm summer night, the kind that is quiet on this highway. They smelled a fleeting smoke, a fireplace somewhere out here, the air made them gasp, quieted them. Ghost giggled; a gurgling, spitting giggling. "Man, man, did you see his face?" The air from the window made Bedri aware that he was sweating, his face was cold, dripping ice. The smoke from the fireplace somewhere drifted to them and left them. He opened his eyes wide to focus on the road. He'd found the 401 somehow, turned west on it towards Toronto and driven into the express lane. The highway sound of cars grrred in his left ear, he liked it. It drowned out Ghost's giggling.

"Fucked up. Fuck up. Fucked up, man!" Ghost was talking to himself. "Fucked up bad."

"Shut up!"

"Man, he didn't want to give the shit up!"

"Shut up, Ghost . . ."

"Shut up?"

"Yeah, we got to think, right? What to do."

"Do? We don't got *nothing* to do. Don't think too hard, thug. It's easy like that, man, easy like that. Fucker should have given it up."

"Suppose . . ."

"Suppose nothing. He should have given the shit up."

Bedri didn't know how to feel what he was feeling. Ghost seemed happy, really high. He should be happy, he should be stoked. Was he dead? His body, big and soft, felt bigger, softer. He took one hand, his left, off the steering wheel, there was something wet on it. Then he felt like gagging. He wanted to scream and gag. He put the hand out the window and scraped whatever it was off the door-frame. He let out a scream that the highway ate, the whimper at the end slid up under the wheels.

"That's what I'm saying!" Ghost responded to Bedri's scream as if they were sharing the same feelings. Bedri looked over at him. He was on a joyride, the thing they just did, and the thing that was supposed to make him feel high too, he couldn't bear the thought of it.

"Let's get some dope, man. Let's get a beer," Ghost said.

"Sure," he said weakly. "Sure." He drove himself off the highway.

"Don't punk out on me man, don't punk out," Ghost said. Bedri said nothing. Three hours ago that would have pissed him off, three hours ago Ghost could never have said that and got away with it, one hour ago. He felt his big self getting smaller as if he was sweating himself away. The man's face, a small scar, a moon scar already on the cheekbone. One minute he was pounding the man's face into the pavement, next minute he felt nauseous. How many guys had he landed his big fist on? From grade school to now. Even Ghost. He had beaten him up. All the time. When they were living raw on Gerrard Street.

Fuck that guy, fuck his face. The guy had thought he was hardcore, but Bedri made the moon scar on his face turn crimson. His father, he thought of his father. His father would say, *I pay, I take shit, and look who you turn out to be. I stay in camps, I lose everything.* His father loomed over him, grabbing his face, squeezing tears from his eyes. *I lose everything, for you to shame me.* When did his father stop saying this to him? When he, Bedri, loomed larger, made a bigger shadow over the dinner table. That was the way it was. A bigger man overshadowed a smaller man. That was all.

"Where we going, man?" Ghost grabbed Bedri's shoulder. Bedri had steered the car down the Allen Expressway and west onto Eglinton Avenue. The rush of the highway subsided here, dismal shops blinked dimly, the dry cleaners, the wig shop, the barrel store, the patty shops, the curtained shadows of regular life moving in the apartments above.

"Montreal ... Let's go to Montreal. It's tight there." Ghost was still stoked; his hand on Bedri's shoulder carried a current. Bedri felt his neck heat up from the touch. Hot moonlight, hot smoke, he thought, electric index.

"Montreal," he repeated the word. "Montreal, yeah, maybe. It's tight there?" There was a childish note in his voice, not the way that question should sound, sleepy and as if he was about to cry.

"Don't fucking bring me down, guy. Let's do this." Ghost thumped him with an elbow. "Let's get some gas right here, right here!" Ghost pointed to a gas station on the left.

"Okay, okay. I can see." Bedri pulled into the station and climbed out of the car. "My father ..." he said for no reason, and walked toward the street. Ghost got out and pumped gas into the tank, all the time calling Bedri from the station. "Hey. Hey, hey, B!" When he put the nozzle back into the pump he signalled to the man behind the glass in the station's small shop that he was coming and walked toward the street. "Don't lose it, man."

Bedri said, "My father . . ."

"Nobody don't know nothing, guy."

He followed Ghost back to the car and waited while Ghost paid for the gas, and when he came back he said over the roof of the car, "I'm going home, Ghost. Take me home." Ghost said nothing but got into the driver's seat. Bedri stood outside for a moment then got in. They drove back onto Eglinton, still going west.

"My father is going to kill me." Bedri finished the sentence he had been trying to make at the gas station. Ghost chuckled and when Bedri looked at him, Ghost raised an exaggerated eyebrow. "Just saying. He would kill me."

Ghost sucked his teeth in disgust. "So what, guy? So fucking what."

THREE

No misunderstandings, no embraces. No kisses, no fledgling love affair. No late nights when Jasmeet's voice would call up to Lia begging from the street to throw the keys down. She was always forgetting or losing her keys. And Lia's feeling of being clear and open for the first time? A casualty. Just like their meeting, their friendship, their near love. Brief.

It occurs to her that you can go to sleep at night as one person and wake up the next morning as another. It occurs to her that you can go down into the subway at Main as one person and emerge at Lansdowne another.

That's probably how Jasmeet disappeared. Simple transposition; she went away and when she tried to return she was someone else.

Lia is listening to Rudresh Mahanthappa and Bunky Green. She likes music without words. This music makes her feel ubiquitous. Bullshit she tells herself. After all, she can't reach Jasmeet, and ubiquity would be able to help her do that. Ubiquity could find anything. She has gone by all of Jasmeet's haunts, the Ossington galleries, the late night diner on Dupont Street, the Fusion Underground Club on Augusta. No one knows where Jasmeet is. No one's heard from her.

This is how they met. Lia has hauled the garbage bags with her belongings up the stairs to her new room. She's figuring out how to turn the key in the lock when the next room door opens. The smell of lavender and marijuana fills the hallway. Someone like her, like her age maybe, like twenty, except not like her, dressed like … crazy, rushes out. "Hey," she says, glorious smile, "I'm Jasmeet, your new best friend. Can you hold these keys for me, please? I'm always losing keys." Lia forgets her own business, drops her bags, reaches her hand to Jasmeet, takes the keys, then they both laugh. Instant.

The rent hasn't been paid. The landlady, Mrs. Cho, knocks every day at Jasmeet's vacant room. Lia is on the lookout for her, she listens to Mrs. Cho come up the stairs and when she knocks on Jasmeet's door, Lia rushes out saying, *Jasmeet is sick, Mrs. Cho!* when Jasmeet isn't even there. *Have a little patience,* she tells Mrs. Cho, *have a little compassion.* She fends off the landlady for quite a while with the sheer will of her expectation that Jasmeet will be back. She'll be back, Lia tries to convince herself. A little patience is something Lia knows about, a little patience is the substance she deals in.

Hence Lia's theory of transposition. It happened so fast; one week, two weeks, four weeks have gone by since Jasmeet left town. Lia is biking now along Bloor Street, going east, no hands, her coat is open like a sail. It's Jasmeet's bike. She's keeping it. She doesn't stop for traffic lights. Choruses of car horns follow her. At each block she becomes someone else, some other part of who she might be. One block she's carrying flowers, one block she has newspapers. At the university she thinks of cadavers and at the museum an emptiness swaddles her. Then the naked mannequins in the posh shops embrace her at Bay. At Yonge the perennial road and construction crews offer her graves that will open annually.

Lia knows Jasmeet won't return. Not to this spot, she won't. So this hanging on has been really her refusal to admit her loss. It's just that she can't believe it. Jasmeet had called her on the way to Pearson Airport, then she'd called her from the airport before boarding the plane. And then the last call, two days and ten hours later from Cuzco. Since then, no call, no text.

It's her own fault. Jasmeet had tried to convince her— she could have gone with her but she's tied by the ankles to this city. Tied to her brother, Germain, and her strange mother, Mercede. So Jasmeet left. That's not why Jasmeet left for Peru. No. She left to find a desert, she said, to find quiet, and to journey on ayahuasca. *They say the desert is the quietest sound in the world, taking ayahuasca leads you to a pure-intentioned love. I understand,* she'd said when she phoned from Cuzco, *I don't blame you. We all have our paths, Lia. I feel the earth breathe here, and energy, so much good energy. Your qi is blocked,* Jasmeet told her, *there is a negative energy hovering around you. Everyone has to love themselves. You can't believe it here, each moment is sacred.* Lia heard the desert in the ear of the cell phone. She heard the quiet that Jasmeet heard then Jasmeet rang off.

The hallway fills now with Lia's regret. If you came to her door, you would be blown against the opposite wall with the force of this regret. Lia jitters on the doorstep of Jasmeet's locked room, she has the keys but she doesn't tell Mrs. Cho. So no carpenter will bring his tool belt and tool kit to the room for weeks yet. And no desperate student will view the room—the paint splatter, the unwashed dishes, the clothes on the floor mixed with hammers and paint, and fabric with globs of dried dye. All these are remnants of Jasmeet's performance pieces, her interpretations of Oshun, the goddess of beauty; Kali, the goddess of wrath; Bellona, the goddess of war. Jasmeet was interested in goddesses. Jasmeet was *on a path away from corporate shit,* she'd said.

Needless to say Lia continues to ring Jasmeet's cellphone. No answer. She imagines her calls bouncing off satellites, the great telescopes of the desert, the Pleiades. She's sent texts—after the first week: "How is it? When?" Ten days later: "If you tell me where you are . . ." Next, after three weeks: "Mrs. Cho freakin' out." She's called Jasmeet's parents; they become as anxious as she is. Now Jasmeet will hate her for alarming them but Lia doesn't care. Lastly, after the fourth week: "I'll be on the island!"

On weekends, she and Jasmeet had gone often on the ferry over the lake to Ward's Island. She had loved the lake putting volume and distance between themselves and the city. They would walk naked, where you could walk naked, on the beach at Hanlan's Point. Jasmeet, decadent, except for beaded strings around her waist and *mehndi* on her hands and feet. The last time, Lia had asked to borrow a waist string and Jasmeet had removed one and placed it around Lia's waist. *Wouldn't it be great to live here,* Jasmeet had said, and Lia agreed. Jasmeet had talked about her travels through the world so far, going to all the spiritual places. She'd already been to Varanasi, went to *aarti* on the ghats for five nights and bathed in the Ganges. Then she went to Rishikesh and studied the Bhagavad Gita with Swami Sivananda. It was such a relief to listen to Jasmeet. Like breathing air. She was like someone from another world. So far away from the world Lia was used to, a world full of the emergencies of a small life. Jasmeet had said these places were power places, where the magnetic fields were strongest and she could feel their sheer power pass through her, and now she wanted to go to Peru for the Mayan apocalypse. Everybody was going, she had said, and Lia should go too, to recalibrate her qi.

Mrs. Cho's certainly wasn't a 'power place,' no magnetic fields above Dundas street. The only phenomenon registering over the cracked ceilings, the cracked linoleum, the peeling paint in the hallway, is Mrs. Cho's quarrelling: *These young people. Artists! Always short with the rent. They always want light fixtures fixed and toilets fixed and hallways swept. They want snow removed when it piles up at the bottom of the door. They are lazy and don't do it themselves. They leave the door open when it snows so the snow rises one flight of stairs. They think it's funny. Soon, soon . . .* Mrs. Cho threatened. Ward's Island. That's a power place, Lia thinks. She'll find a place there and when Mrs. Cho sells the building it will probably be replaced by a condominium, like Jameet said. They'll wipe away any sign of Lia and Jasmeet and put hoardings up advertising tiny overpriced units.

Corporate shit, like Jasmeet said.

Lia only has small desires: like finding a first true frie? like waiting for Jasmeet to call up from Dundas Street the keys. And for weekend nights in drum and base d clubs, and rides on the ferry together away from th? But mostly she wants not having life change up on the time. As in the life she'd had before. When th?

Jasmeet was ahead of her already. They could have been lovers. She should have gone but she didn't. Sometimes you have to catch a feeling right away, but nothing in Lia's life so far has made her trust this idea.

FOUR

All cities are ambiguous and not just in fog or snow or rain. There is sometimes the inability to make a thing out. Fog, here, can make the next block a mystery, snow disguises the known topography. And rain, something a poet once called the happiest of weathers, rain can make life doubtful. Anyway such is the changeability, the indefiniteness of this city, a plain day is never plain. So even though it's summer, it's that kind of a day in the city. In fact it's not quite day. Everything is still perfect. June sits up in bed. She's heard something on the radio that wakes her. "One hundred musicians?" she says. "Great!"

DIONNE BRAND

"Musicians? *Policemen.* One hundred *policemen.*" Sydney's been lying beside her, awake, contemplating the highway commute. She rolls over, places her feet on the floor.

"He said *musicians.*"

Sydney laughs, "Sweets, you're still asleep, dreaming."

"Pianists, maybe then, that would make sense, I swear I heard pianists."

"Heading to Jane and Finch?!" Sydney laughs again.

The radio's red numbers burn the early morning dark of the room. June is positive. The radio show she wakes to every morning on CBC never fails her. It said one hundred musicians or pianists or flautists or guitarists, but definitely something to do with music.

"That's going to be amazing."

"Dream on. You think they're sending anything but cops up there?"

June feels as if she's inhaled water. God, the idea of one hundred musicians in the Jane-Finch neighbourhood! Fucking perfect. "It's genius!" she calls to Sydney who is moving toward the bathroom.

"For crime control, June. Why the hell would they send one hundred musicians?" Sydney's voice is slightly exasperated now. She turns back to June on the bed, just to make

28

sure June's not talking in her sleep. June's hair is in sleep disarray, her hands in a splayed open gesture. June is sitting straight up and now she sounds combative, "Why not?"

"You're kidding me, right?" Sydney only wants to go to the bathroom, shower, get on the 400 and get to work, ninety-six kilometres north, in Barrie, on time. Sydney doesn't want an argument, especially not a ridiculous one.

"I heard, distinctly, the city's sending one hundred musicians to Jane-Finch. You didn't hear it, so don't just dismiss it."

Sydney really just wants to say, *good morning, honey,* and decides to say, "Good morning, honey."

"Don't be patronizing," June says, "I'm only saying 'one hundred musicians' is what the radio said and I think it's a brilliant idea."

Sydney looks at her patronizingly.

"Okay, fine," June says, "listen, they'll repeat it, you'll hear."

"Honey, it's extra police for the gangster shit up there, it's not kindergarten."

"Musicians," June says emphatically. She's intransigent now.

It's too early. Sydney doesn't want a fight. It's five-thirty in the morning. The sun's not even out yet. If it shows up at all today. There was thunder around four a.m.

Sydney remembers that once, June spent all of breakfast, the whole bloody morning, talking in Tamil. That was because the before lover was Tamil. And once, in the middle of the night June woke in Spanish. That was because of the Chilean lover in the 70s and the Nicaraguan lover in the 80s. So now these musicians. Was June seeing a musician on the side? June carries remnants of people, of things, of the world, with her. We all do, but June carries hers on the surface, her skin is iridescent with these glimpses and glances. And certainly her dreams are lustrous. Where others would filter out, June takes in. She never says who she really is though, or how she arrived in the city. Maybe she was born here, maybe not. Perhaps when she arrived she was carrying so many remnants that her true self became obscure to others. She's vague about her past but she's curious enough about other people's. Sydney suspects her of polyamory but wouldn't dare ask her. Anyway, if she did, June would say something vague or something that felt like knives and that would be the end of it. June can be vague and then again can be something like knives, and sometimes Sydney, being the lover, wants to risk all of it, like now.

"Okay, let's listen." Sydney sits mercilessly on the bed. Though actually another half hour can't be wasted like this. Already cars heading north on the 400 are tight like a huddle of penguins, the 401 highway running east and west is buckling with steel and rubber megadytes, but living with June is not like living in the real world. "It's policemen," Sydney says resolutely.

"Musicians," June says childishly.

Sydney is becoming intolerant. "What would musicians do?"

"Play," June says. "Soothe the turmoil, calm the heart. Those 'gangsters' are children, they're wrecked. Music would make them happy."

"Don't be naive. They're gunmen. They're sending police for the gunmen."

"The gunmen are children. They need music. They could use some bicycles, some painters, some soccer balls, some fucking trees. The place is pure postindustrial dreck. Who wouldn't want to murder somebody? A hundred trees, a hundred teachers, a hundred trips out of there, a hundred anything—not a hundred policemen. Why are you so fucking pessimistic?"

Sydney has lain down and has nodded off through this bizarre dawn inventory. The word "pessimistic" pierces her senses though.

"Pessimistic! Me, I'm pessimistic! Lord, why am I having this conversation?" She springs up.

"Yes, pessimistic! Why would you say 'one hundred policemen'?"

"I'm not saying it! He said it! The guy on the cee-bee-cee!"

"No, he didn't. You did. What are they? An invading foreign power? For god's sake, they're children! They're suicidal, nihilistic, but they are *children*."

"Murderous, more like it," Sydney says under her breath. Sydney never expected to wake up in the heat of a guerrilla war. Who does? Unless you live with June. June's voice becomes hectoring, "You really don't understand these things do you? Beatriz would."

"Oh fuck, here we go with Beatriz again!" Beatriz was the Nicaraguan.

"But …?" Sydney hears a suddenly plaintive note in June's voice but will not be taken in and bolts for the bathroom. June turns up the radio, waiting for the news.

"No imagination … none …" June is capable of this harsh tone as regards Sydney. She is ruthless when she wants to be right.

The voice begins reading the news and June raises the volume again. It says, and June unquestionably hears, "The mayor has decided to send one hundred musicians including flautists, guitarists, bassists, saxophonists, drummers and pianists to the Jane-Finch corridor of Toronto to help curb the violence in the neighbourhood. The plan was approved by City Council . . ."

"Yes!" June yells toward the bathroom door.

People hear what they want to hear. Right then Sydney is thinking, June hears what she wants to hear, believes what she wants to believe. As if she's not living in the same time as the rest of us.

On a wall in the bedroom, there's a picture of June dancing in a park among a troupe of dancers. The men are dressed in black, the women, including June, are in orange. June was sixteen then and thought she would dance on Broadway some day. She isn't yet who she is now.

Even back then June's righteousness was patent. No one told her secrets, perhaps they saw perpetual virtue in her face, as if any failure would shock her. None of the women among the dancers trusted her. They had secret lives she suspected, lives secret to her at any rate. She was aware of these secrets, though not in any concrete way, but by the way conversations stopped when she approached, and how their laughter seemed to contain the esoteric knowledge of some requisite carnal pain that her laughter lacked. Her demeanour stopped anyone telling her a dirty or dark secret; no one confided any sordid material in her. She felt anxious, always, as if she were forever missing out on the details of what was happening in front of her very eyes. Her face was too reflective. It bothers June to this day. Her face is still a liability that way. She was also, back then, very impressionable, and perhaps she still is: she only has to hear a word or see an image or have a word conjure an image and she will be taken up with it for days. So the dancers weren't entirely wrong in not confiding in her. All their confidences would have stayed with her; scored her. June cannot ignore hard things. Not June then, not June now. But June back then was in her timid life, and dancing was her greatest rebellion.

She remembers the day in the photograph, the sun, the orange skirts of all the other women and the music. Trevor is beside June in her orange skirt. He is young too. He is bare chested. Nothing hidden or sad about him. He is open, naked. All his desires are on full display. He wants to dance through life. And he will. He parties all night, sometimes with the other dancers, the women, sometimes on his own. He comes to class with a smile saying, "Oh, I had a terrible night," his hand over his eyes, his mouth grinning. His terrible is joyful. He is always looking for drama, for fun. He got June and the other dancers in on starting a speak-easy with him. He thought it could be a speakeasy at night and a dance studio in the daytime, and he could also live in the back room. And they did that for a while. But the dance studio didn't work out: none of them had any money in those days, the ceiling was too low and he could not jeté around the small room. But he was saving to go to New York to try out for the Alvin Ailey American Dance Theater. He was going to leave the city because there were only small parts for him and he was going to New York, which was bigger and lighter. June remembers him so well, bright, glittery. His body gave off sound waves. You could see all the graceful mechanics of his skeleton. He was like a taut wire dressed in muscle, but his humour made him pliable. He loved himself, he loved his arms and his legs and his neck and his torso.

He treated June like a little sister, though she thought of him as less mature. What he knew was sensual, but her budding politics told her that would not be enough for her. When he came into the dance studio he always had a wondrous story. Things always happened to him unexpect-edly, he never knew why they did. But they were always extravagant. He used to live with an eighty-year-old Russian woman who said she used to be a dancer too. She never made the Bolshoi—she said, instead, she was in the ballet in Bologoye, a town between Moscow and Leningrad—but she knew everything about dance. She was small and slight but commanding, and Trevor loved her. She taught him the engineering of his body and which muscles to use and when. He thought that she was cute and funny and charming because she told him lascivious stories about life in Bologoye; about sex in the train station with strangers passing through. Galina, that is what she called herself, Galina. Galina did not like June. Galina did not like many of Trevor's friends, or so June thought. Galina wanted Trevor all to herself. June noticed that Galina never took her eyes off Trevor. She drank vodka martinis and curled herself on a couch directing him here and there to bring her a scarf, bring her a martini, rub her poor feet, give her a kiss. Trevor teased her, telling her not to be so jealous and attention-seeking. When Trevor moved into the speakeasy June asked him what would happen to Galina. He laughed and said, "Oh, she'll find herself another boy soon enough."

Here again, June did not understand the mysteries of intimacy, the mysteries of a woman like Galina, or, as open as he was, a man like Trevor. Now June would say, it's not the mysteries that she doesn't understand, it's the conventions she refuses. She had first met Galina when Trevor invited June and the other dancers to Galina's small cottage in Cabbagetown to watch pornography. June went feeling that if she didn't it would confirm all their assumptions that she was either naive or a prude. And she was not a prude. Trevor made martinis, which June had never had. Nevertheless she drank three in a row simply to seem sophisticated. Trevor giggled and told her she was cut off. Galina chuckled in a self-satisfied way, as if June had finally proven how gauche she was. June averted her eyes from the pornographic screen when one or another of them wasn't looking at her to see her reaction. She was embarrassed and bored at the same time. She could not feel aroused as they all seemed to be by the spectacle, and it seemed to her farcical, the pumping of penises into vaginas. When June said this aloud, the dancers all said that she was not an adult, and Galina and Trevor laughed and looked at her with pity. There was no reason, June thought, for Galina's derision. What had June done, except be young, that Galina hated? What had she done except dance with Trevor, except have young, strong legs, except have an erect backbone where Galina's was turning to powder?

When Trevor broke off with Galina, June noticed all the time she had spent taken up with Galina, and how Galina had insinuated herself into June's daily thoughts. It was jealousy of course, jealousy of an enigmatic kind since neither she nor Galina ever had sex with Trevor, but their claims on him had a sensual charge. All sex is not physical, June knows.

June left the dance troupe because she couldn't fly. She woke up one morning, a morning just like this morning with the radio, and thought, "The end of dance is flight and I can't fly." Trevor could fly. He could soar across the studio. And he was heading always to New York. He laughed at everything. June remembers his laugh, like some cascading bird laugh with a gurgle in it like a baby's. When he left for New York she felt as though she'd lost something—a big part of the day, a chunk of air. He left her his clay dishes, his clay jug, as if giving a child a sweet to hold her until he returned. June has pieces of those clay dishes even today. In that picture where June is dancing with Trevor, and the troupe, the sky is wide open and blue to all of them. It's summer. July. Energy is burning in their torsos. They were about to go on tour, they were about to break open the world of dance in the country, they were all beautiful, black hair, black limbs, red beating hearts. After the dance they were going to wander around the crowd and drink some wine and lie in the grass.

FIVE

"It's another country." Ghost.

"It's not." Bedri.

"Trust me, it is. I went there once."

"You never went anywhere."

"One time. I went one time. 'You can't just be cool, you have to know shit.' That is the only good thing she said to me."

"Your mother?"

"Yeah. Mercede. So trust, I know shit."

"What you see there?"

"Things . . ."

"Things! I know you didn't see *nothing*. You don't even know the way."

"They talk a different way."

"Talk a different way? Who don't?"

"You're an asshole, they talk a different language. They got French."

"Ghost, you're the asshole. I knew I shouldn't have gone with you." Bedri's sentence hung on the windscreen. It was the first time doubt had sprung up between them. Through everything. The first time, real doubt. Not just daring or put down, but doubt. *I shouldn't have gone with you . . .* Their friendship hung in the sweating air of the car, rough and harmful.

It was four in the morning. They drove west across Eglinton quietly, even carefully, after that revelation. At a stoplight, a cop car rolled up alongside. Even this they took calmly. The cop car turned right on Caledonia and they took that calmly too. No deep exhalation of relief, no triumph about how close that was. Bedri lifted his elbow to the window, his hand to the upper frame. His hand felt heavy. He looked at it. His hand was swollen. It was heavy and swollen.

"Stop here, here!" Bedri said. They were at the inter-section of Eglinton and Keele Street, nothing there except

a car wash, a string of low-slung buildings ending in a convenience store, and a high school. Miss June, he thought. A
small light over a door next to the convenience store showed
him the tag he'd made in bold black on the door a year ago.
It was a Drop-in centre. "I won't make you scrub that off
if you learn this," she'd told him. She handed him a poem
by Xavier Simone. He read the first lines and smiled. It
jangled in his head now. Love Poem 17. *But I am going with you,
love / I hope you remember the suitcases, fragrant / with books / let us
meet in rain-drenched cities / let us meet smoking cigarettes / let us take
Urdu dance lessons / let us arrive in Arabic on Monday.*

"Why you wanna stop here? The Beast's gone." Ghost was
glad of the broken silence, as if they'd returned to their old
selves. He pulled over. Bedri opened the door, got out and
walked back toward the light post near the school at the
corner of Keele Street, lifting his hand to see. It seemed
deformed to him. Deformed as the man's head, and broken.
There was a small smudge on the knuckle of his index
finger, and his nail on the little finger, the one he kept long
and polished, was broken and hanging. He hadn't noticed
that before. He pulled the rest of the nail off and felt a
short pain as his right hand seemed to pull itself away
from more beating. The pain travelled to his elbow and he

dropped his hand, placing it between his legs, bending over.

Ghost sat waiting, the Audi humming. He looked in the rear-view mirror, watched Bedri raise his hand to the light, and then drop it between his legs. He pressed the gas, bringing the car to a low growl; he hoped Bedri would respond to it, turn and come back to the car. The traffic at the intersection came and went, cars peeling off Keele Street heading down the hill, or gliding past them along Eglinton. But the two of them existed unaware now of the rest of the city. Unaware in the ordinary sense of being aware, of having somewhere to go, or return to, someone to call. Not that they ever had someone to call, except in an emergency, but now they had no one to call; not even in an emergency.

Bedri turned towards the car, walked back, opened the door and said, "I'll take it here, dude."

"What you mean?" Ghost said, looking straight ahead.

"I'll take it here, I'm gone."

"We ain't nowhere, here," Ghost said. "I'll take you home, no problem, Money."

Bedri's hand hurt. He wanted to say, sure. He heard the begging in Ghost's offer. He saw the nub of the right side of Ghost's neck scar.

"No guy, it's cool, I'll take it here." He shut the door,

turned toward the light pole again and walked in its direction. He heard the car linger, then rev up and take off. His hand hurt, but by impulse he lifted it to wipe his face and doubled his pain. He leaned against the post. He didn't think of Ghost. He thought his hand was broken, and how would he explain it? How would he explain it to his father? Fuck.

A thief is always under suspicion. A coward is full of precaution. In the ocean one does not need to sow water. Poverty is slavery. He who does not shave you does not cut you. A brother is like one's shoulder. One cannot count on riches. To be without a friend is to be poor indeed. Dogs understand each other by their barking, men by their words. A madman does not lack wisdom. A person stands next to shade, not next to words. Where I make a living there is my home. Your woman should be in the house or in a grave. His father told him these things. Now these things ran through his mind.

His father, Da'uud, was a cab driver. He drove a taxi from four to midnight each day. Then he sat in Bilan café with other insomniac taxi drivers till three or four in the morning. Then he drove home across the Humber River to North Etobicoke and fell asleep as soon as he walked in; dropping his dead body on the couch. The living room had become his father's bedroom. His father couldn't sleep in the bedroom upstairs anymore since he couldn't make it up the stairs. In any case, the bed upstairs, he complained, hurt his back. Heavy brown drapes were always drawn to keep light out of the living room. The family only saw the living room on a Friday when the father didn't work but observed the Jumu'ah.

Now his father would be at Bilan drinking Turkish coffee and smoking a cigarette. There would be other men there, his uncle Abdi Fateh, his cousin Ghedi. It's where Bedri should be too. His father kept insisting that he go into business with them, drive taxis across the city; learning street names in that pharyngeal sound of their language. Bedri couldn't bear the thought. He'd seen his father once too often sitting at the café, sleep drugged, the smoke of cigarettes crumpling every man's chest at the counter, the brown smiles as they reminisced about some long ago thing, in some long ago country. His cousin Ghedi was a fucker. *Ilkacase*, they called him, lovingly. Khat-eater. Always showing Bedri up, sitting in those old men's laps like a dog. They weren't old men really, his father and his uncle, but they seemed old because of how their life was. It was all in the past tense. And when they told him what he should do, he felt as it they were welcoming him to some petrified life. So he had separated himself from them, separated himself from the grim warmth around the counter at Bilan. He felt left. Even more left now, now that he had told Ghost to leave him here under the light post.

Bismillaah ar-Rahman ar-Raheem, Qul a'uudhu birabbil falaq, Min sharri ma khalaq, Wa min sharri ghaasiqin idhaa waqab, Wa min sharrin naffaathaati fil 'uqad, Wa min sharri haasidin idhaa hasad . . . *I seek refuge with the Lord of the Dawn from the mischief of created things* . . . He whispered this fragmented prayer against his hand. *And from the mischief of the envious one as he practises envy.*

His father told him these things. Why did they come to him now?

SIX

The final decision and the telling had been shitty and abrupt. "No," Lia had said.

"I thought you said, like, you want to. To have experiences, right, like …" Jasmeet said, surprised and disappointed. "Life was too small, you said, right?"

"I don't …" Lia's reasons dried up.

"You agreed, like we said, unlock the beautiful. Think desert! Think Machu Picchu!" And when Lia was silent, "You've never even been on a train ride! Come on!"

"No, no, I really would, you know … I'd like that, I want to …"

"Let's go then. Ayahuasca is sacred medicine, like the sacredest, like totally, they say you see galaxies and you see your heart and it's only the size of an atom."

"I can't. Mercede might . . ."

"Mercede! She's lived her fucking life. Shit, she's a constant emergency!"

"You don't know anything about my mother." Lia had closed down the conversation with this and therefore there was pure silence after. She had found a way out. At first when Jasmeet had asked her to go with her she could not identify the tug she had felt. Suddenly, there was Mercede in her heart, like a heavy rope. How would Mercede get in touch? What would happen to Mercede? So, the inevitable word out of Lia's mouth was, "No." And it had sounded so awful, it had been so involuntary, it was so resolute it pained her.

You have to survive people. You meet people and sometimes you have no control of that, and then it's a simple matter of waiting them out. Your parents, for example, you are in no position to avoid them. By the time you meet them it's too late.

Lia had survived Mercede. Mercede was Lia's mother, Lia's and Germain's. Mercede was wild. That's what Renata said. Renata was Mercede's mother. Mercede was wild. But Mercede said that Renata hated her, did not love her, did not love her enough. (No one thinks they've been loved enough.) And this was why Lia and Germain had spent time off and on in foster care, and off and on in peril. Because Mercede said that Renata hated her and Mercede did not want to hate Lia and Germain. So she handed them over sometimes to the Children's Aid Society. Off and on as toddlers they had stayed with Renata also, and Joe, Mercede's father. And then they lived with other people too, and sometimes apart. And months would pass and then Mercede would find them; go and collect them, even if they were with the best kind of people, that is, people who could love them like foster people or as Renata and Joe did. Mercede would find them and drag them away to her 'I-have-a-nice-place' ugly apartments.

Mercede tried very hard at loving them. She had dried out and gone straight, she had found new places to live, she had found religion. She would smile and cover them with kisses and with her shaking hands. And for a little while, a year at the most, the ugly apartment she'd found would feel like a possible new world. She bought them toys, stuffed toys, even after they had outgrown toys. She made a forever Christmas tree that was never put away in order to assure Lia and Germain that this time, love would last forever.

But this was love according to Mercede, her eyes shiny and her voice bright with a tinkling sound. Mercede's love was exhausting because it needed love back constantly. Lia and Germain were children and didn't always know how to love back. They simply knew how to love, and at times they simply wanted to run or play and have love waiting for them when they returned. Mercede's love was a burning, wanting love. Mercede's love could not hold out against her panic of never being loved enough. And so she worried she did not love them enough without knowing how to love them enough according to that calculus. And feeling that she was failing, she would leave for days on end with someone who loved her. She would never bring "that stuff" home she'd say, never endanger her children, never. She loved them too much, she said, too much. Lia and Germain made do in the ugly apartment or at the neighbour's. And if Mercede came home before the neighbour looking after them finally called Children's Aid, Lia and Germain were in for another round of frenzied love, of Pepsi and candy, and new sneakers and haircuts and pizza.

Lia and Germain had come one right after the other

and so they were practically like twins, and like ghosts. "Where's your ghost?" Mercede would ask if one of them was out playing and the other one inside. And then if she found one at one foster care and couldn't find the other, "Where's Ghost?" she would ask Lia. "Where's Ghost?" she would ask Germain. Lia didn't like turning into some-one else, or turning into nothing, she hated that word. Germain took it as his real name.

When they were nine and ten, Mercede took them to Renata, their nonna, and Joe, their nonno. Lia recalls they stayed there for two relatively peaceful summers until the fights between Nonno and Mercede, each time she visited, became screaming and violent. Mercede said Renata and Joe were trying to steal her children from her. When Mercede visited, Nonno changed from a quiet gruff man into a lump of red charcoal. This is when Lia decided she had to outlast Mercede and everyone else. The boisterous cursing fights when Nonno called Mercede *prostituta* and Nonna called Mercede *demone* and Lia watched them while Germain watched the television. Then is when she decided that you had to keep the noise of other people out of you. This is when she knew the only recourse was to watch and wait. Wait, because you can't change people, you can only change yourself. And pray to God to get to sixteen and declare yourself an adult. Lia had done this at last, three years ago. Mercede read the court papers with sadness, relief and admiration.

It seemed to Lia that she saw Mercede between bruisings. Mercede was beautiful and each set of bruises strangely accentuated the beautiful part of her like an accusation. How come she was ruining it, the beautiful part said; how come she allowed it to be ruined, it cried. Mercede chose lovers who could ruin the beautiful. She walked right into them like walking into a wall or like walking into speeding traffic. All of Mercede's men punished her for being beautiful, in the end. And all of Mercede's men punished her in the end for choosing them. These men did not know what to do with beauty; at first they thought it was good luck and were surprised, and then they thought it was bad luck and hated it. The thing is, they expected wealth to come along with beauty. When wealth didn't come along after Mercede, they asked her why; if they had beauty why didn't they have wealth too? These were poor men and even though they thought beauty would be enough, it wasn't enough. Wealth did not follow beauty. Mercede caused jealousy and her men loved that, but when it ran out, they blamed Mercede, accusing her of sharing their beauty and squandering their luck. But what about me, Mercede yelled at them, what does this beauty bring me, assholes!?

Mercede never mentioned Lia and Germain's father, who was one of these men, except to say that he had gone to Alberta to find his luck all over again. He had left a small wound, a leaf-shaped scar, a gingko tree leaf on the forearm she'd raised to protect her face. Lia and Germain don't remember him. When they think of him, because of Mercede's story, a map of Alberta appears.

Where Lia had decided to simply wait out her time with Mercede, Germain wanted to stay in that time until Mercede was perfect for him. The perfect mother. In the end he had the same kind of unassuageable love hunger as Mercede had. The same kind of burning love hollow. And of course Mercede never satisfied it. So it turned into a war of love between them. That meant volatile days, up and down days. They see-sawed, both of them. When he behaved like a good boy Mercede took off with a new love. And when Mercede was straight and sober, he broke bad, bringing the police to the door for shoplifting, for threatening, for spray-painting, for smoking dope. Lia got out of the way of that war at sixteen. She'd spent the last year of high school in a group home, and found a job in a laundromat, then in a No Frills, then in a Wendy's, then as a telemarketer, then in a mall kiosk selling phone covers, then in a dollar store and finally in a TV packaging plant in Etobicoke. She moved almost every month over two years until she rented that room next to Jasmeet's on the second floor of Mrs. Cho's.

And Lia doesn't miss them. Not the way you miss people and want to have them with you. If she misses them, it's the way you miss the skin where you burned yourself and there's a scar now. She doesn't miss the noise of them, the clanging unpeaceful noise. Not a bit.

SEVEN

It's difficult to say anything conclusive about love, but June once travelled on the back of a motorcycle for it. They left Toronto in early August on a humid day. In August, always, there are days of stifling humidity, as if the lake is boiling over. That year the atmosphere was claustrophobic. That was when she had the Chilean lover. It was in the time of Pinochet, and the Chilean had arrived in the city, fleeing. A journalist and a musician, the Chilean was guilty of all the things the regime said he was guilty of. Canada was the only way to avoid jail or death. June was on several solidarity committees for revolutions around the world. Chileno Solidaridad was one, and she had offered to put the Chilean journalist up for a while. This is how things were in 1975 through to the late 80s. This is how you fell in love. You would offer to put someone up, someone fleeing persecution or terror, and the next thing was, you were, euphemistically, sleeping with them. This is how love was then. They say these situations happen in war, when you are afraid—it affects some people this way. Like the way plants flower when they're in peril. Plants flower, people copulate. June wasn't in peril, not actually, but she felt in peril. Everyone felt imperilled at the time. The world was in peril. It still is, but not everyone feels that now. The Chilean was in trouble and June became caught up in the thrill of his endangerment and then one thing led to an inevitable other.

It was the summer too. All June's summers were explosive back then. Vital. She woke up each morning, her brain luminescent. So much to do, so much to think, she put on phosphorous clothing to go out. She misses that. Those wonderful sleepless nights with stunning arguments and dazzling theories and finally falling into bed breathless with fucking, exhausted and drunk on visions about a coming world. Then she felt at the vertex of mind and body.

The Chilean was exciting but not very good at English so June had to learn some Spanish. She liked the sound of the language. And his name in it: Isador. It sounded like "adore." The whole language seemed so . . . urgent.

Sex didn't need English, of course, but love did. And so June couldn't say for certain that she loved the Chilean. Revolutions were so wonderful for sex. Okay, it wasn't that love needed English, per se, but at the time June determined that it needed a common language that wasn't sex. And as much as people might think otherwise, sex is a limited idiom, not a whole language—it gets exhausted. Like a conversation that peters out into what we don't know and can't express. No doubt there are bursts of eloquence, but the prosody isn't always affective. And sometimes, just sometimes, the sex becomes less and less compelling like a stilted idiolect.

Not that June was sentimental or needed or even wanted a sentimental kind of love. In fact, she was a solitary person and Isador's presence in her apartment after a time became tiresome. For example, he hummed when he ate and this was innocent enough and even interesting for June from an anthropological view. She was taking a minor in anthropology and surmised that the origin of this humming might well be found in hunter/gatherer peoples. But that thought and fascination was temporary, as temporary as sex, so the habit began to annoy her after a brief while. And Isador never washed a dish. He smiled his most charming while saying to June, *"Pero mujer, soy un hombre,"* to which, when she could, in Spanish, June said, *"Pero hombre, no soy tu madre."*

After the initial weeks, when Isador's endangered status was the leaven in the relationship, and after a few more weeks when June felt embarrassed that she was growing tired of him, not as a revolutionary but as a person, she began staying out late. Mostly she was at the Sigmund Samuel Library at the university, sitting in the stacks, reading a fluorescent book, *Being and Nothingness* or *One-Dimensional Man* or *Return to the Source.* She was at the University of Toronto at the time doing a degree in political science. The ordinariness of the domestic with Isador dimmed an element of her she wanted to keep, namely a sharpness, a solitary intelligence.

Isador was quite popular—he was not the only revolutionary in town, but he was both dangerous and brilliant. June had hoped to see this side of him more often, but understandably, who can keep that up twenty-four hours a day? Most of us have a public self that may well be sexy and daring and then we go home and flop down on the sofa and retreat into our dimwitted vestigial selves. It is no insult to say that the care and feeding, the upkeep of the human body, the physical self, is not unlike the task that zookeepers have each day. So much forensic effort is necessary to keep this animal at bay—toilets, mirrors, soap and water. One comes upon this presence abruptly when sex wanes or falls away. Especially in a relationship of short duration where one hasn't had the time or compassion to forgive the inconvenient animal in us all.

Montero Baet was his last name and he had worked for *La Prensa* as a freelancer. He was also coincidentally a musician in the university café life in Santiago at the time. The former played only a minor role in the full indictment against him: the truth is, everyone with even the vaguest association with democracy was in trouble with the Pinochet dictatorship and its American friends. It was his singing that got him into trouble, and his guitar. Isador sang songs to friends who had been arrested and disappeared. And when this criminal side of him emerged—he laughed when he said that—people at the university café and the newspaper were detained. He got away.

All this led to June and Isador riding the Trans-Canada Highway on a motorcycle in the summer of '75 on a political tour. Some who know nothing about South America might say Isador was pretending to be Che. At any rate, June discovered she didn't like the wind in her face as much as she had imagined she would. Nor the intimacy of holding Isador around his waist for hours on end. There is intimacy and then there is intimacy. The intimacy of trusting someone with your life on a motorcycle is different from the intimacy of having them enter you, strange as that may seem. And love, love as they knew it, love as she knew it, was dwindling.

They were between Regina and Saskatoon. June saw a horse. She looked back until it was out of sight, though in that terrain nothing seemed to go out of sight. The sky was big and the land went on forever—you could be standing in one spot the whole time. When the horse disappeared June saw a sign saying "Blackstrap" and said to Isador, "Stop." June got off in the middle of nowhere, took her backpack off the bike and said goodbye to the Chilean.

It was a passionate goodbye but she simply had to return to the serious work of finding a job in order to keep the apartment in Toronto and to carry on welcoming refugees from political terror from all over the world. She was never one for small dirty rooms, and the bar life the Chilean seemed to love just turned her off. Isador understood, he too was growing a little tired of this ball-busting *morena*. He set off to write his own diaries, heading west. She waited on the side of the road for a Greyhound. It didn't come but she'd seen the horse. Soon enough the obligatory pick-up came down the road. By ways and means, June passed through Bladworth and Davidson and Craik and Bethune and finally Regina where she took the Greyhound and slept intermittently until Toronto. Between Regina and Toronto there are long monotonous stretches of road, and she would disembark into whatever town or city along the way, buy coffee and get back on to the bus heading east.

Back in the city, from time to time she heard from Isador who had kept going till he came to Vancouver. There he had met another June or perhaps Julia and settled in. Over the years she learned that they had moved to Victoria and had children. What an escape, June thought.

June worked El Salvador and Mozambique, South Africa and Zimbabwe, then Nicaragua, putting up one revolutionary after another and getting rid of them by all sorts of means. She was, in this way, in terms of love, in terms of sex, indiscriminate. The Nicaraguan, for example, was a cigarette-voiced *clandestina* from Estelí. June was electrified as Beatriz gave an intense speech in a church hall on Bloor Street. Everything about Beatriz was covert, esoteric and riven with intrigue—the way her gaze summed June up in the fifth row and settled somewhere around June's lips before moving off again. June was jealous when Beatriz's eyes moved on and settled on someone else. But they returned and stroked June's throat. Beatriz's voice was like sandpaper and after that occult interrogation the whole speech was merely a love letter to their impending affair. This was a woman who woke up with a start at one a.m. every night searching for a revolver. Or at June's neck hoarsely asking, *"Quien te mandó y que quieres de mi?"* Who sent you to me, indeed.

Why, why did she always end up with some frightened person in her bed? June had decided not to think too deeply about that. After all, sex was just sex and there was no need to double think it unless you were Catholic or born-again Christian, and June despised these ideologies. If not for the paranoia, and perhaps because of it, Beatriz was the only one June considered keepable. Beatriz had her own life and her own thoughts and wanted nothing from her. Assigned to international work, the Sandinistas called her "undisciplined in the field." The fifteen thousand bombed by Somoza in Estelí had turned Beatriz's blood to adrenaline. That would drive anyone mad, June reasoned. She was so fierce she had become a liability to Ortega.

She had been decommissioned to diplomacy. Beatriz disappeared, naturally, leaving cigarette burns on the floor beside the bed. She was going to finish the Somocistas off, she said. *Quien, Quien te mandó?* Who sent you to me?

When Pinochet was eventually deposed, and this was seventeen years later, Isador appeared on her doorstep. He arrived at the Women's History Archive where June worked, and she did not recognise him. He looked like a placid man, his cheeks had puffed out, his mouth opened to an avuncular smile. Not the half smile he'd had to the dangerous left side of his face, not the tight jeans or the tight body. Maybe that was all fear back then. It makes some people skinny, the nerves eat away at fat then at muscle. This Isador looked well-fed and happy, content. He said he was going back to Chile, taking his children to see where he was born. He hoped it hadn't changed and he hoped that it had changed. He came with a little bunch of roses. How sentimental, June thought, then restrained that bitter side of her and thanked him. And why did you find me, she wanted to ask, and what on earth would we have to talk about now?

June, despite what she thought of herself, was simply utilitarian. She could not understand the finer sentiments of regular people or a concept like friendship. And so, especially when she'd had sex with someone, the warm seconds of human understanding that the other person may have added up, the tiny affections for inclined heads and dimples, the expressions of love, these nostalgias escaped her. So when Isador referred to their time together, which did indeed amount to seven months, and his gratitude to her for helping him through the first months of his life in the country, June was embarrassed. She would never have taken her Chilean for this kind of man.

"I wanted to see you before going back to Santiago. To thank you."

"No need, Isador . . . it was the struggle . . . you know, *la lucha continua*." June tried to laugh it off but Isador persisted. Obviously he had created a story where she, June, was some kind of heroine.

"*Pero* June," he said, still pronouncing June with an "h" sound at the beginning, "*Pero* June . . . you saved my life . . . I loved you." In the face of this declaration, what could June do? She thanked him kindly. There was another uncomfortable moment when she did not follow her gratitude with a reciprocal declaration of love. Even love past. His love hung in the archive. June didn't know what to do with it.

It was not that June was not a warm person, or a generous person, or a kind person. Her love was simply bigger than the personal. It was bigger than the love individuals have for each other. Not to put too fine a point on it, if she did love Isador, it was not Isador personally but the revolution Isador represented that she loved. She loved the idea of people rising up against injustice and political terror, and insofar as Isador did this, she loved him entirely. This impersonal love, this political love was for June a deeper love, a more democratic love, the ethical love.

"*La idea es*, June," he added, and she recalled learning this from him. "*La idea es* . . ." meaning anyway, whatever. "Would you like to come to Chile with us? You are my family too." June had to put an end to this. He was going too far. Imagine she, his wife and children going to Santiago together—how awkward. Ridiculous. Not because there was anything between them, but on the contrary, they were strangers.

"Isador," she said, "my work here is very important," sweeping her arm in a gesture that took in the shabby office of the Women's History Archive. "I cannot leave it, we have a crucial campaign coming up." She said this to be kind to Isador and because his request had made her remember why she had taken him in, apart from the sex. Of course there was no campaign, June's political actions had become smaller and more personal. Her only activity now save working at the archive was a youth Drop-in, in what they called an at-risk neighbourhood. Maybe, she'd thought, maybe with kids, she could begin the process of human liberation sooner. Though actually kids did not need liberating except from normative training. So it was an anti-colonial project of a sort to defend children from the state. The state was merely a dominating machine, anathema to the whole idea of a liberatory life. So Emma Goldman had said, and June was reading Emma Goldman's *Living My Life*, more closely now.

There had been three revolutionaries: Isador, Eliazar and Everado. Dangerous as they all seemed, only Isador had looked her completely and freshly in the eyes. This she'd always taken as a sign of his honesty, even though she came to learn and despise his sloppiness later. The women who took Everado home ended up being beaten. Some had mused at the time that Everado had been brutalised so much that he thought it was common manners to do the same, but June thought this kind of justification was bullshit. Eliazar had a wife in Germany and perhaps that might have been the more economical choice to make given that any encounter would definitely be brief, but Isador had had the clearer eyes.

Isador was placated by June's explanation and June invited him to lunch to shore up the notion that she was not being harsh and inhospitable or ungrateful of his gesture. Lunch could only be a half hour, she said quickly, forestalling the possibility of a tedious time. Half an hour took two hours all together as Isador went through photographs of his family and his life. June was genuinely interested, marvelling at the great change in him. In the end it was as if she had never known him.

Sometimes people are so utterly different from one year to the next. If June had seen this Isador years ago, she would have fled also, admittedly. Still she would have been more sympathetic maybe. Perhaps, she thought, perhaps it is not so complicated, seeing that human beings themselves are not complicated, just their ability to discern is compli- cated by all the signals they have to receive and send. Some prehistoric June was always in the process of calculating light, and flight, the sensory information necessary for surviving. And so easily one sensor or one feeler can be off. And June's sensors were invariably off a degree or two. So back then she only received a certain signal from Isador, the way one receives, through light, the colour yellow, but not its ascending colour orange or the descending colour green. That is, she had seen him from a particular angle, as if she were standing at the angle of thirty-seven degrees and Isador at forty-five. She saw his flat underside but not he himself. Isador was in a similar position yet of course different. So he would return years later with a small bunch of white flowers and a placid face. And June at thirty-seven degrees still, would gesture to the shabby office and decline. But perhaps if they had seen each other from all angles none of this would have happened, not even their first meeting. We do what we can with what we have at the time, even when we believe we are trying to break the angles.

Beatriz would never show up with flowers, June thought. Beatriz was serrated, another geometry. *"Olvidate que me conocias,"* she'd told June. That could not be mistaken for anything but what it was. Forget you knew me. Perfect. Though June felt slightly imperfect at the time, slightly miffed that she wasn't the one telling Beatriz this. Of course that was ego—but perhaps it was love too. Because, after all, isn't love absence? Like the absence of a limb makes you notice where it was and what it did. Beatriz had been very obtuse and suspicious. And there were reflexes to her that June did not want to travel. The nights Beatriz didn't wake up from sleep violently at her throat, she had insomnia and lay there smoking beside June. She was the type of woman you should ensure leaves you, rather than the other way around. That way she would not hunt you down.

EIGHT

*S*ome *young men your age are making jihad, look at you. Nothing.*
Gangster, what is that? No faith, no nothing. I wish you would
wear a vest with bombs rather than being a thug. You waste my life and
you are a shame in the face of the prophet. I waste my life here for you.

"You want me to make jihad? Eh, Dad? You making
jihad doing taxi?"

To tell the truth this is a city built for winters. In the
summers Toronto sits disconsolate, humid in its thick pink
fibreglass insulation. This is what the father, Da'uud, thinks
and he thinks this is how his children have become, built
for winters, thick and with a rough, abrasive inside. They

are dull against his words, his barbs. He is not even a religious man. At times he is harsh with them, he says things
he doesn't mean. He cannot make that Bedri do anything.
He has invoked the worst curses against this winter boy,
ciyaal baraf, this boy who grew way beyond the height of the
doorway and the width of Da'uud's hand.

"In this city you have to keep your belongings with you,"
Da'uud tells this to a woman in his taxi. He tells her
everything about the boy and everything about himself;
how he was an economist, how he trained in Switzerland
in 1978. How many languages he speaks, Italian, English,
Arabic, French, Somali. How he went back home and how
in 1994 he fled. The whole country fell apart under the
men who knew everything. The military men, the religious
men. The hard men. "You've heard this story?" he asks
her. "Before you know it, you're trapped. Five languages,
Miss. Five."

She is looking out the window along the lakeshore. "No,
that's terrible," she says. Why do men force their lives on
me, she thinks.

"Yes, terrible," he says. "So I tell him all this. He doesn't
care. He can't understand."

"Hmm," she says.

Da'uud picked her up on Eastern Avenue and he's driving her along the lake as it wanders in and out from view. "So where are you going, Miss?"

"Nowhere, really," she says. She's vague. But the man she is meeting has told her she is beautiful.

"No, Miss, I mean the address. Where you call the taxi for to go." He drives past the island airport with this red-haired passenger. Does it matter who he was before this? No, it doesn't. The day he stepped into this cab it ceased to matter who he was. The day he set foot in this cab his life, so to speak, changed.

"Sunnyside," the passenger says.

"Sunnyside," he repeats. "Sunnyside," he repeats again. The woman is brooding, so he is quiet. Every six months there's an inspection on this car, he has to do this to keep the plates, then there's the gas, then there's the other driver, who is always crying about money as if Da'uud doesn't have enough children of his own. Of course this is not what he would have done if there was any other way but there was no sense thinking about that. The heart is sore. Before you know it you've been driving a cab for ten years. The cab flies along the lake at the south of the city to Sunnyside.

"Where in Sunnyside?" he says when they are near to Parkside Drive.

"Just here," the passenger says.

"Here?"

"Yes, here. The parking lot," she says.

He pulls into the parking lot. There are geese crossing the lot going toward the lake. Da'uud waits, the geese cross. He wishes he could come out of this cab and walk with the woman. She pays him, he sighs. It would change his life again to go walk with her. She waves to a man near a statue. Da'uud glimpses the man's face. He doesn't like it, it tears a sliver in his chest. He thinks, that man can kill someone. He has seen the faces of people who can kill people. The woman flutters toward the man. Da'uud leaves, saying to himself maybe he's wrong, the things he knows are not useful. None of the things he knows has helped him to recover Bedri as a son, an obedient son whose life would redeem the choices a father makes.

The lake oscillates like green-blue wet glass. What is in that lake, the woman leaving the taxi wonders. She wonders this the second after she sees the man's face. After the taxi pulls out she walks towards him. She's dyed her hair red for this meeting and she hopes he likes it. She's met him here before. He always seems furious at seeing her even though he's called her and begged her to come. Once she sees him she always, for an instant, regrets coming. But now she sees the lake and understands her attraction to him. She thinks, there is something turbulent there but she can't see beneath the surface. Like looking in a mirror.

The geese go about their daily life.

The woman and the man walk toward each other expectantly, and then they turn together along the boardwalk toward the Humber bridge. All that they each had rushed to this appointment to say has evaporated. It has become inaudible or unspeakable. It walks between them, a slim column of molten air. They cannot reach through it to hold hands or embrace, its particles are prickled like small spinning blades. She has nothing to say to the man and the man has nothing to say to her. What is in that lake, the woman wonders again. She wishes she could see through its billowy green. A bird, red under the wings, flies across their path and the woman says, "Look!" She wants their meeting to be full of wonder so again she says, "Look!" She wants him to see the red underwings as an omen. But he ignores her. He doesn't want to see anything beautiful. She tries to touch his arm, the spinning blades sting her and she withdraws, then she turns again, gripping his arm this time so that he stops, turns toward her grimacing, feeling the blades cut his wrists and his forearm muscle, feeling himself a casualty of an event, though of what event he doesn't know.

He cannot fathom why he brought her here, why he wants to hurt her, why he wants to hurt himself, to crush something in himself. It is not love that brought him here, it is possession. It is not love that brought her here either, it is possession. It is so private, so sacred, so over-whelming, this possession, and it is malignant. Possession covers their heads, it is a tight band, a cupola of airless air. A covering so complete there is no world outside. Except she sees the billowing lake and she wants to dip her head into it, she sees a sign in the black bird with red underwings and she tries to show him. While the man is thinking that if he can free his forearm or if he can absorb the pain he can surface. Otherwise he will pull her down with him, and he doesn't intend to go alone—he knows he is selfish but he doesn't care. Why should he go alone? Why should he have to take all this hatred with him and leave her in the beauti-ful world? Then she will live without him and forget him and who is she to have the world while he loves her, and while he is gone.

Months ago he had spotted her in a bar, no, it was out-side a bar in the Distillery District. Despite its condo reincarnation, the old Gooderham and Worts factory lay its 19th-century shadow on their meeting. He was smoking, she was smoking, though it was freezing outside. He wasn't lonely that he can remember. He was sad, but he is always sad. The kind who has a primeval sadness, before he was born he was sad. No, he doesn't know why he is sad. When she gave him a light he wanted to speak Dutch to her but he didn't actually know Dutch. His mother knew Dutch, his father knew Dutch, but he didn't, he only knew English, so he started off wrong with her. He said, "Hey," and that was the beginning of misunderstanding. He couldn't get the right language out of himself, he only had feeling to go on and feeling is all primitive. That night he told her he'd been a peacekeeper, first in Bosnia and then in Haiti and he showed her how to subdue someone. He grabbed her arm and twisted it and then he let her go and laughed. She stayed talking to him after because she was afraid to walk away. And because he said she looked like Hilary Swank, and then he said, "Hit me in the face. See if you can do it." And she did.

People can't handle the senses the way animals do. Animals eat, drink, sleep, fuck at a certain time. They don't kill if they don't have to kill for food. People have no borders, everything is mixed up, they're lawless. Both of them were lawless. And it had brought them to the lake. He said she was beautiful and she took his statement as a command and did anything he asked. She had no centre except that word. She had been hanging from that word ever since she was a child. It meant giving other people pleasure, saying "yes" and never "no."

The woman loves being loved, more than she loves. That the man loves her is more compelling than whether she loves him. But sometimes, as now, she is overwhelmed by this love and breaks off to the lake or to the red under-wings of a black bird. The blades cutting into him are spinning deep. He pulls his arm away and is about to hit her. Then the chamber he is enclosed in opens a fraction and he hears "butterflies."

"What?" he screams at the woman.

"Nothing," she breathes. She ducks her head and crouches down. He feels someone run up to him. She sees two women run by briskly in an argument. His arm arrests mid-stroke, he brings it down on his head and walks off. He's sure he heard her say "butterflies." What butter-flies? The woman is still in a crouch on the boardwalk. She's going to stay there until he's gone. Then she will find the taxi man if he's still there and she'll go home.

That is what Da'uud, the taxi driver, saw, the possibility of violence in the man. He's seen this possibility in people all over the world. Beginning in Mogadishu during Siad Barre's time and after he fell. It was there. The lethal tensions in the city. It was no longer important that he was an economist: the economy had tanked and now faith was the engine. He saw the signs: he saw the disrespect from ordinary people, and that it was more important to pray than to think. He had lived his life until then on the falsity of the idea that prayer was all that was necessary, yet he knew how powerful that idea was: it made people irrational and murderous. But then the facts of his profession glared at him: it too was irrational, though disguised as rationality; it too was murderous. How many eventual deaths had he relegated to one side of a ledger, calling this act "austerity"? The kind of murder that was gradual. Not the sweeping murder of the famine or the war. But at least, at least, he thought, his kind of murder was accidental. All murder was bloody but when people murdered for faith it was elemental; it was crude and bloody. He wasn't capable of that, others were capable. The brother of his wife had wrapped himself in robes, joined the faith courts and become capable of anything. Da'uud had thought that bailing out of Mogadishu with his wife and daughter would be enough.

But it wasn't. Everywhere the violence had assailed him. When they arrived in Addis Ababa and later in Rome, it was there too—this same violence of faith—in people. He toured a church in Rome. It was full of ferocity and punishment. All he saw there was more blood. It surfaced again in the airport in Sweden in the simple look of a border guard, the interrogation room, and as much as he tried to ignore it, the violence pursued him over months in Oslo as he searched for work and a place to live. It made a dull sound like a weapon, a cleaver, on a human back.

This is why he is talkative in his taxi. He watches the road and he talks as much as he can. He doesn't want to see that violence in people. He talks even faster when he glances in his rear-view and sees someone like the red-haired woman in the back seat. He wishes he had told the woman he dropped off at Sunnyside to be careful, but nobody listens to him. Not his wife, not his daughter, not his son, nobody. Well, perhaps his wife, Amal. She listens. She left Mogadishu with him even though her brother was against it. If not for her the brother would have killed him. And look now, that same brother has sent his son to Rome for his education. So much faith, so little faith. After they had made such a mess of Mogadishu, a mess. He could have told that woman, he could have told her, but who listens to a cab driver; who listens to a man from another world.

The lake is green this early evening, Da'uud notices. He began noticing the lake after three years in the city. Before that, life was like a hand over his face. When he discovered the lake he tried to get all the fares along the lakeshore. He likes this end of town, the south. It has definition, it has nature. If he is to drive a taxi, to spend his life driving a taxi, he'd rather drive it here along the expanse of the lake's shore, from Cherry Street in the east to the Humber River in the west. You don't see nature much in this city, not from a cab. Unless nature includes people. But he tries not to get involved in the passengers' lives, he tries not to feel their anxieties. *Insha'Allah.* He's got anxieties of his own, and that kind of nature he can do without. The day driver loves people, or so Khalid says. Khalid is always talking about how good people are, how funny, how crazy kind they are. Maybe, Da'uud thinks, maybe day people are that way but not evening and night people. Maybe the day driver gets more sleep so he has a better perspective on people, a different perspective. Da'uud doesn't get enough sleep, but that makes him keener, he thinks, more alert to people. He only sees evening and night people and while people can be pleasant enough in the daytime, at night they run amok.

Da'uud would rather be in an office with numbers and papers. He does not want to embarrass himself, he does not want to embarrass his family but ... and this "but" always sits on his chest. He has a good life here, there is nothing wrong with working. Poverty is slavery, and one cannot count on riches. There was that "but" again. You live, you live. You get married, you have children, you make a family. Nobody says how, just that you have to do it. Which is what he told Bedri. You live, these things you do. He even sent Bedri to Somaliland, where it was calmer. To see how life may truly be lived. Because despite everything, there you meet your obligations and you live a good life. It was over for him but not for Bedri.

Five airports from here to Somaliland. Dau'ud told Bedri, you will pass through five airports. Each one a passageway to how life is supposed to be lived. In the first airport, Pearson, you get rid of all the things you are living. You remember but you can forget it because you must leave. You are sad, you think you don't want to go, because of the people you leave behind. You are anxious. You want to hold on. The left side of your chest is raw with this, maybe. Yet you are not so sad because you are a little excited for the future. You escape into that fact. You must do this, you must. You are being made to leave. In the airplane you already feel a little far away from yourself. You are only yourself because you know that you are yourself. In the second airport, you are a small book with a coat of arms at the wicket before a guard. You are a photograph and a hand under a glass window. He looks at you. He does not recognise you—not the you you know, nor the you that you are leaving behind. He, the guard, is looking at the new you he makes with his stamp. You see your self in his eyes now. After you pass him you are even less the self you know you are. In this second airport—it could be Frankfurt or London; it might be Paris—you get rid of the other half of what you were living. After all, you are only a passenger, you have the portable body of a passenger: it only holds what it can carry. In the third airport, Abu Dhabi or Dubai, you remember nothing. Falling asleep, waking up on a bench, listening for your flight, you are suddenly blissful. You feel free. All the things you were worried about in the first airport, the friends you left, the events, the work undone, all this is irrelevant. They have gone away. You are in the middle of time. You can do nothing about old friends, they don't matter. The thought occurs to you in this airport that all the important happenings you had planned, all the anxieties you experienced living in your life before the first airport, it's good that all this does not exist. You need no longer exist in that life. It is going on, without you. You get some water now, you eat something, you hear your flight called. In the fourth airport at Addis, your eyes are open, your ears are open; you smell the world. You can change your clothes, free your legs, you can melt into a new life. You take out a phone from your pocket, you do not recognise it. It is your old phone with numbers from your life before. Is there someone you would call there? No. So you throw the phone away and you join the new ways of the people entering this life: how easy it is to forget, you say to yourself. You laugh. Hargeisa is the fifth airport. It is raining when you arrive there. There's an earthy smell in the air, the smell of cool rain on the hot ground. The rain is not heavy. You breathe in the open world before you. Your bag of clothing and all that you thought you needed seem weighty. You're tempted to leave the bag but you are vaguely curious to see what the other person who was you some hours, perhaps a day and a half ago, has in that bag. You're sure you have no use for anything in there except perhaps a toothbrush and that you can buy. Here is your new life. You know no one and no one knows you. You will make no mistakes here and all past mistakes are erased. You begin.

When you return, if you return, you never return the same. And where you return to is not the same.

He is my boy, Da'uud thinks, but he has no imagination. Bedri returned from the African continent and slid right back into his bad habits. He was new for a while, full of all he had seen and learned from the five airports, but after only a few months, the city seeped into him once more. He became friends with that boy again.

Lake Shore Boulevard stretches in front of the taxi. The dispatcher has been calling him. He hasn't had a fare since the woman. He's just driven this line of lake and rail and condominiums and old factories and beaches for the last hour, thinking.

NINE

Every other Wednesday, Sibyl, the woman who washes her face in Clorox, came to visit June at the archive. She washes her hands in Clorox too, and any other part of her body that she decides needs it. Clorox, Sibyl said, was a great invention and if only Lady Macbeth had had it, none of us would have known that story. June pointed out to her that *Macbeth* was a fiction, only a play. But the woman said it had to be true first, for it to have become a fiction.

She came to see June about dreams. Was it possible, Sibyl asked, was it possible at all, that she was in a dream?

This question gave June real pause. In reality she should tell the woman no, no it is not possible. But why? The woman is delusional, but what good would it do to tell her that? It would be much better for her if it were possible that she was in a dream. The reality, in which she washes herself in Clorox, is much more understandable as a dream after all.

So June told Sibyl, "Quite likely." Sibyl looked relieved, briefly, then looked at her bleached hands. They were dry like papyrus and some parts were burned white. "And how do I stop dreaming?"

"Well," June began, "I suppose wake up."

"But I don't . . . I can't now." Sibyl turned her attention to a brown patch of skin near her left wrist and began brushing it with her right thumb. The small brush strokes would turn into rubbing in a moment, and then she would need the key to the washroom to go scrub the spot fully.

"Dream something else then," June said.

The woman's thumb hovered over her wrist, she smiled at June. "Yes, I can do that. I think I can do that. I've had many other dreams, you know, lots of others."

"Choose one then, Sibyl." June's voice urged enthusiasm. "Choose another one."

"I had one where I went to the mail and found a package

and there was a rubber band around it and I took it into my room and opened it and inside there were three gold keys. I didn't know what to open with the keys. I left them in the box for a day and lying there, they looked like bright metallic babies. But they were not babies. They were metal keys, gold shiny keys and each had a red ribbon—and did I tell you about the buds of flowers in the box, they were metallic too. What does it mean, do you know?"

"I'm not sure," June replied. "Should it mean anything?"

Sibyl rubbed the palms of her hands together. The Clorox made them itch. June heard her pop psychology tone and felt a small self-disdain. She had not anticipated that sentiment in herself. She was not a psychiatrist, she was not a counsellor, the archive did not do that kind of work. Gloria, the head archivist, became agitated when Sibyl came to see June. After Sibyl left, Gloria said to her, "This is not Queen Street Mental Health."

June and Gloria were the only employees at the archive. Not exactly employees, they were a collective of two, recording women's social action in the city. Gloria was a historian and June, of course, the social activist. So naturally they would clash, though they were perfect for an archive. One, to rush madly in, the other, to pull the brakes. It wasn't their job to save any one woman, Gloria said. "Big Picture, June."

This was an archive of feminist social history. A hot arrow flew up June's nostril. Yes, and Sibyl is a casualty, June said bitterly.

By way of history, which is really allegory after all, June's father had told her, "Only read the business section of the newspaper. *That* is the news. The other parts are the casualties." He had said this to her from the veranda of the house where he lived with a second family. It was where she had discovered him quite by accident one morning when she was late for school and took a shortcut down an unknown street. He did not explain the identical house with his identical chair and his identical glass of whiskey on the identical banister. When June arrived home that afternoon, there he was in the same position, it seemed, with the same advice in her own house. That time he added, "The other parts are the casualties and the fantasies." Her father was a bright man haunted by certain failures; certain situations that should have gone his way but didn't. June and he found solace in the business pages of the daily newspapers. He taught her how to read the architecture of a society in the printed word of passing governments and rising industry. He had been promised a job by a politician for pulling in votes in their area and he had been totally ignored after the man's victory. That was in another country, another city. And June has stored this information like a jewel in a safe. Her father might have failed personally but not politically. That is, he had been correct about the world.

Sibyl appeared a week later to report to June on the progress of changing to another dream. She was trying to settle on a dream strong enough to displace the Clorox dream. A dream such as that, as everyone knows, has to be fairly powerful. It had left her with papery, itchy skin and various compulsions. She was forced to carry around a bottle of Clorox on all her journeys throughout the city, to scour subway seats, to spray bus shelters, door handles, money boxes and railings in the streetcars and buses. She had adapted one bottle with a spray mouth for easier use. Such a powerful dream needed a replacement more powerful still, since it had virtually taken over her entire life, to the extent that Sibyl was besieged by her impulses. She felt responsible for bleaching the entire city. "Who sent the keys?" she asked June, "Did you send the keys? When I touched the first one last night it softened and bent."

"I didn't send the keys," June told her, and then she asked the woman, "Did you see a door anywhere?"

"I told you, there's no door." Sibyl was radiantly annoyed with June.

"Well," June said, "I think you have to find a door for the key."

"Anyway, forget the keys, they don't help. There's no door I said!" Sibyl glowed with anger and then subsided. "I'm here about the magnesium and mercury. I have to swallow magnesium and mercury and everything will turn out right."

"Who says?" June asked. Why was she in this negotiation, this relationship, with this woman?

"Do you know where I can find magnesium and mercury?" Sibyl asked. That's all she wanted, June now saw. She had lost credibility asking about a door.

"Mercury is not good for you," June said, "they've found it in dead fish."

"You don't know that for sure, do you? You're not a scientist, are you? You don't know anything. The magnesium and mercury drink is not poisonous for me."

At this difficult point, as Sibyl got up to go, Gloria walked by the door, her head rigid.

"Dream something else, Sibyl." June was desperate.

"I have to go," Sibyl whispered. "I'll tell you how it works out."

Where Sibyl spent her other days June did not know. Sibyl detailed her dreams, not her whereabouts. She must live somewhere, June thought. She could not live on the streets, her Clorox fetish would not work there. Sibyl had told her she'd been thrown out of several shelters because of her habits, compelled as she was to sanitise each space she occupied and the paths leading to it. She had tried to adjust. She carried small perfume bottles to disguise her Clorox. One small green bottle from Christian Dior, one atomiser from DeVilbiss, one Givenchy bottle and one eau de cologne by Elizabeth Arden. She showed them to June as you would jewellery, a certain pleasure beaming through her damaged face. These bottles, of course, were not hers to begin with—she'd acquired them through various means June could only guess at. The atomiser was Sibyl's favourite—she did tell June she had swiped that one from her last job. She'd emptied the perfume, which she thought stank, and filled the bottle with Clorox. It wasn't very large but it was elegant and she hoped people appreciated that elegance: there were two Greek women reaching for a god on the bottle. Sibyl had been fired for its disappearance, though they could not prove she had taken it. The world is unfair, she told June, they did not prove it, yet they fired me. They should have to prove it.

Magnesium and mercury. June hoped no place was mad enough to sell the woman mercury. Magnesium was harmless enough, though she didn't know what it did in great quantity. Perhaps if Sibyl remained preoccupied with a search for mercury it could replace the Clorox fetish. She might let the bleach fall away as not effective, and of course no one in their right mind would sell Sibyl mercury.

Perhaps it was memory loss Sibyl wanted. Mercury would do that, displace all the good minerals in the body and induce memory loss. Or perhaps Sibyl wanted to slow down the energy, the adrenaline she devoted to cleaning and disinfecting herself and the world from whatever disease she thought they had. Sibyl saw the invisible diseases that were quite possibly there.

You never know who you'll meet in this city. Apart from the constant construction and reconstruction occasioned by winter, there are the appearances and disappearances of people. One could, as is often the case, disappear into someone else. One could become totally invisible. And so Sibyl disappeared, became invisible after that last visit. June looked for her and waited for her. She prided herself on knowing the city, but Sibyl knew it much better and disappeared. June checked the shelters and the vans that served the homeless. She went to Lansdowne and Bloor, the corner where she'd first met Sibyl, where Sibyl had first hinted at the realities of dreams. Once or twice she thought she caught a glimpse of her, but hurrying quickly to meet the figure it would turn out not to be Sibyl. Who knows who she may have disappeared into. Perhaps she had become a dental assistant, to find mercury. Perhaps she found the door to the key and walked into another life.

Sibyl's dream keys had stayed in June's mind and puzzled her. There were three gold keys, Sibyl had said. June wondered if they stood for time or simply the letter "k," which needs three gestures. June could not believe her own ineptness. She had tried to play about in someone else's life without having the wherewithal let alone the imagination. People think they can save other people but really they're trying to save themselves. Now June understood that she had to figure out what part of herself she had been trying to save when Sibyl approached her.

June hates referencing her own biography, she thinks that when people do this they draw false parallels. Her mother was a cheerful woman. A woman who did not want to know very much except that life was good. And so June never told her of meeting her father on the veranda of that identical house on another street. Later June abstracted that her mother probably knew, but did not need it confirmed: it would have spoiled her mother's sense of goodness. And still later June thought, why must such arrangements always appear as betrayal? It was a betrayal by her father, of course, but only in the context of totalizing it as a betrayal; that is, of having that set of emotional formalities laid out in that particular way; that teleology, if you will, of domesticity.

June doesn't believe in a codex of childhood events that adjudges the state of one's present life. She knows this is the way people think they come to "understand" things about a person: this is what they share in coffee shops and in bed together, and this is what they extrapolate into friendship and familiarity. Not her. She rarely offers her lovers a catalogue of her past or her childhood. Now is now, she thinks. Here is here.

But perhaps she had caused Sibyl to lose faith in her who, in hindsight, read Sibyl's dreams literally. Key, door ... June was slightly embarrassed for weeks after Sibyl disappeared from her. She spent three weeks looking for her so that she might redeem Sibyl's faith in her, to offer some other suggestions for the presence of a key—or three keys—in a package. She had forgotten, of course, that when you are not in a position to order your life, disorder has its own order. Which is not like the disorder of order but like the order of disorder. People with ordered lives, as June's was relative to Sibyl's, have nothing to offer people whose lives are in disorder. They moralise and psychologise and proselytise and pretend they know, but that is their own anxiety and impatience. They have no idea about disorder. It is a different country. A different set of principles. And people with ordered lives always think that people whose lives are in disorder are looking for their kind of order. They think their kind of order is happiness, when their kind of order is gluttony and selfishness. And with all this order, June thinks, we are creating wreckage and disorder, piling it up like a midden.

Things don't remain the same in this city. Perhaps Sibyl froze to death in an alleyway. June has been keeping an eye on those statistics too.

TEN

Perché non hai tenuto di più a Mercede? Perché non hai tenuto di più a Mercede? Perché non hai tenuto di più a Mercede?

The older woman watering the porch stops to look at her. "It's you?"

"Yes it's me, Lia."

"Well, so it's you then."

"Yes it's me."

"Gesu Cristo."

The hose falling limp from her nonna's hand squirms and bounces, the water uncontrolled. Lia points to it, leaning Jasmeet's bicycle on the tree in the front yard, then runs down the side of the brick house on Russett Street, to turn the tap off. When she returns, her nonna says again, "So it's you."

"Yes, it's me."

Renata is wearing a house dress, a pair of slippers, some old-fashioned glasses, and now she places her hand across her chest. Lia goes back to Jasmeet's bicycle, she holds it like a fence. She says to her nonna, *"Perché non hai tenuto di più a Mercede?"* She has learned this sentence by heart. She's practised it in quiet moments for years. She knows no other sentence in this language. She doesn't know what she expects to happen after she's said it. She expects a heart attack. She expects a fall to the sidewalk. She expects a change in the amount of oxygen in the air. Her grandmother drops her hands in a gesture of supplication. That's all the Italian Lia knows. *Why didn't you love Mercede better?* Even if Renata answers in that language, Lia would not understand. She only came to say this sentence, to register it, to have it said.

There, it's done. Lia climbs onto the bicycle and takes the first step on the pedal. It levers a gushing of Italian from her grandmother. It begins softly, pleadingly, and becomes louder and more rapid as Lia pedals down the sidewalk. She looks back. The early summer envelops her hair, her articulating legs, her shiny face. She waves and waves as if to say see you soon, until her nonna is lost in the curve of the street.

Renata looks down at the hem of her house dress and the hose fallen from her hand.

She is not an old woman. In her own head though she remembers the day she became an old woman. It was the day Mercede left home. Everyone thought of her as an old woman after that. She might as well have been a widow—no daughter, no future wedding, no son-in-law to be proud of. Shame. In her head she is herself. Renata. That self before Mercede's rebellion. In the life everyone sees, she wears house dresses peppered with little flowers, from the stores on College Street. Dressed like this, she sweeps the veranda endlessly, extending her long brush strokes to the sidewalk and to the sewer drain. But in her head her legs are bare, her face is rich, *ricca* and smiling. The girl, Lia, hadn't seen that, she'd only seen an old woman sweeping. She wishes she could have shown Lia the woman in her head; the woman who thought Mercede was right to run off, she was right to go dancing late, she was right to wait until they were all asleep, pack her things and run away. Live. But she was also the one who never, ever, said so to Mercede. She was jealous of her daughter—and she was afraid of that thought. She was paralyzed by Mercede's going and then all the blaming—from her husband, Joe, from the neighbours. She had to defend herself, so she bought some of the flowered house dresses that everyone wears and buried Renata, the jealous one, inside. Then the neighbours left her alone—and by that time Mercede was truly lost. When Mercede reappeared with first one child then another and all the troubles, Renata was grateful she had another chance. She bore it all, the coming and going, and Joe's cursing.

The paragraphs gushing out of Renata as Lia set Jasmeet's bike in motion is all about that, all about being incarcerated by the house dress, the way the waistband makes her helpless and the prints of flowers—or geese or flags or teddy bears—make her dizzy. She was not the devil, she loved Mercede as much as Mercede would allow and as much as she herself could.

But Lia is riding away, she cannot hear that Renata loved Mercede, even loved her for her wildness, for living life as if she did not have a set place, an obligation. If it was up to her, she would have run away too, lived a life of fierce self-will and self-destruction. A woman should have that right too. She didn't know what had kept her feet pinned to the ground. Or truly what made her go and buy the house dresses from the small stores on College Street to harness that impulse. It was a leaden part of her brain, a part that could not wake up no matter how she tried to pump blood to it. It was the civilised part where she knew for sure something like an animal slept. The feral part would never have done that, it would never have gone down to the store with the pots and pans and the house dresses hanging outside and grabbed a handful off their hangers. That part of her brain, the animal part, would have run away with Mercede. She told the girl biking away all this, she told her it wasn't any justification, it wasn't any excuse, it was what happened. Lia was dragging this account away, it trailed behind the bike in a long streamer, and Renata kept talking along this lingual trail. *And where is the boy?* she shouted after her. *Where is your brother, Germano?*

Her declarations seared her throat but they kept her attached to the girl, and maybe the girl would take them away with her along all the streets. Tell everyone. How long Renata stands there is indeterminate. How long does anyone stand where they have to, in order to explain incidents in their life and exonerate themselves? How could she know that today the girl would come and unpin her? Someone could make a painting of this, the older woman standing near the house with the words coming out of her mouth, stretching to the wheel of the girl riding away. It would be a vague summer day, a slight wind would turn the long streamer into waves. The house dress would dissect and hold one of Renata's arms aloft. Her face would be young. Lia's face would be an owl's with glasses. The bike would lift off the street as Renata's news takes air. Lia won't look back but she can hear the rustle of explanations. A surrealist painting. A Varo painting perhaps. It redraws events. There are possibilities here that neither the girl nor her grandmother have thought of yet, though they may desire them.

When Nonno died, Mercede arrived at her father's graveside weeping and yelling, *"Figlio-di-puttana!"* Renata fainted. Mercede continued screaming hoarsely. Lia and Germain, fourteen and thirteen, were stricken, they began pulling their mother away whereupon she wrenched herself from them and sprang at Renata, choking her until they were able to drag her off.

Mercede lives in Hamilton now, Lia takes comfort in that—close but far. At the head of the lake, at a distance, enough rope between them, she had thought, until Jasmeet asked her to travel with her to another world all together. Mercede said Toronto had too many temptations, but the truth was Mercede had run out of temptations in this city. She wanted, she said, peace—though, Lia thought, sooner or later Mercede finds noise. But at least in Hamilton it would be less. It was smaller, Mercede said, and she was sick, sick of people in Toronto. Lia had no idea who these people were but she was glad of them, she liked the new location of Mercede sixty-six kilometres away. And it was strangely soothing hearing Mercede's scrambling half-there voice on the phone every two weeks or so saying, "Yeah, you okay, sweetie?" As if Mercede could do anything if Lia wasn't okay. "Yeah, Mum," Lia would reply. "You okay?"

"Oh yeah, yeah, can't keep me down. You know life is never easy, you know. You know, *figlia*, anyway . . . Eh, you seen Germain? He's not here, eh. Took off, you know that. That boy . . . Whatever did I do . . . ?" Mercede would peter out this way. Lia would stay silent. Everything between her brother and Mercede was incendiary. He had moved with Mercede to Hamilton but as usual it had blown up between them. Lia stayed out of it because though the two of them fought like bees, they would turn on you if you attacked one of them. Finally Mercede would begin again cheerily, "Anyway, so you're doing well? Good for you, sweetie. You were always the smart one. Always the smart one. You take care, you take care. Talk to you soon, eh? Nice. Nice . . ."

Life is never easy. Funny, Lia thought, how she could hear the sound of love slowing down in Mercede. And funny how it was that sound that kept her roped.

ELEVEN

Summer. Kerria japonica near the front steps, in full aureolin bloom. It's Sunday morning and on the living-room couch June has just come awake. Outside, across from her house, in the west end of town, is an ubiquitous alley-way. It's Sunday there too. Though you wouldn't know it. There are three guys jittering around and for them, specific days don't really matter. One day flows into the other. They decide when it's morning or evening by the foot traffic of customers or the sirens of police or something more subtle than that—something most other people don't think about or know about. They inhabit another kind of diurnal, where the prickly feeling of reality, of the real, jerks you awake. The sensual nature of days, their dimming and lighting, don't concern them. Neither does the Gregorian calendar: the body is its own calendar. A certain weather of the blood claims them, a circadian alarm clock depending on the chemical composition of the blood, but not just ordinary blood, blood augmented and accustomed to whatever drug has been ingested for however long. So it is that kind of a day.

The living room is lit by daylight. There is a brown rocking chair, a television dominating the room, June's body on the couch. Her lower extremities are still asleep, her brain struggles to be awake. Outside the light is shimmering bright, blinding. It's summer, though it is winter in the alleyway. The three guys shivering there can attest to this. No, it isn't the sun glaring off snow. No, there isn't snow on the pavement. The alleyway is not an icebox as they will swear to you it is. Their weather, winter, is tingling under their skins. There's a medicine for the weather in their bodies and they are waiting for it.

June slept on the couch because there's a young man in the bedroom upstairs. She's known Bedri for a year and a half now. June loves children and children love June. She thinks of them as children but the kids who hang out in the Drop-in aren't really children, they're teenagers with little room at home and less on the street. June can't help but feel, as with her friends in the dance troupe all those years ago, that she doesn't know half of what goes on in their lives. Bedri's not a child but he's a child to her. She made him learn Xavier Simone's "Love Poem 17" when he tagged the Drop-in doorway with the Arabic letter for 'b'. Then she had him recite it to the heckling crowd of his peers. She knows he wouldn't have done it if he hadn't wanted to.

The thought of Bedri makes her swing her legs to the floor. But the room seems dark to her until she realises she has her sleeping mask over her eyes. She giggles and lifts the mask off. The room is bright and blinding just as the day outside. June lifts the window curtain. Across the street in the alleyway, three men are leaning on the railing looking down the street. They're early today, they're waiting for their dealer. Jesus, June thinks. What time is it? She switches the television on to the weather channel. Nine-thirty a.m., 22 degrees. She turns the TV off, peers out the window again. The three men are pacing now, a fourth man in a grey and red windbreaker has arrived. He passes out small bits of aluminium foil; he seems jovial, brisk. The four men hurry deep into the alley and stoop down, the fourth man leading. I should call the bloody police, June thinks. But she remembers Bedri upstairs. Not that they would know that he was upstairs, but perhaps they'd want to come in and she couldn't let them. She'd drawn the story out of Bedri little by little over the evening, clarified it with what she'd read in a garish column in the newspaper about inter-gang violence. She had been unable to condemn him, or tell him to leave. She made an ethical decision and that was that. It would be a betrayal on two fronts, she'd told the kids her door was always open, always open—she'd been warned not to cross this line but she had, fine. Second, she had no intentions of enabling the police state in any way. As Emma Goldman said, as long as people were *living a life they loathe to live* then crime was inevitable. She only saw a sweating boy last night through her screen door, a young man others in the city would see as threatening because of his height, his sullenness, his lurching walk, his clothes, baggy. "Self-protection!" she said, "Can't you see, Sydney? They themselves are afraid for their lives!" She was naive, that's what Sydney said. "You have absolutely no filter. It's as if your skin is some kind of litmus."

"Well what is your filter? I'd like to know."

At a street festival last summer—it was going on evening, it was a Sunday—she and Sydney saw a small family, a woman, a man and their daughter. It was only a short moment but June caught them looking into a shop window, and it was the way they stood, more than anything, and the face of the small girl. She had some stringy shoes on and a pink dress and June caught a certain look in her face. It was a desire that would not be satisfied, as if the man and woman had made a vain promise to the small girl, a promise they would never fulfill. So the girl has a future happiness on her face, but even she understands the futility of it. It didn't matter what was in the store window. It could have been a pair of shoes or a doll or a dress. It was an object potent with their inability to have it. June was immediately pained and perhaps it was this pain that made the family weak and desperate too. They turned away from the window as June passed and they all looked at each other, they seemed caught out, as if June's presence had exposed their poverty, their weakness.

She remembered her own childhood and just such a store. The store was no bright place either, just a discount place, not a posh window. People like them did not have posh tastes, they had shiny tastes or practical tastes and neither could be satisfied. Someone was always taking desires and making them expensive and out of reach, making you linger at the store window on a sad street and long for nothing.

When she was a child she had stood at such a store window and seen a black pair of patent leather shoes with a strap over the instep. And so catching sight of this small girl she felt a melancholy. She had quickly looked away from the family, but that moment lingered with her all day and for some days to come. Sydney would tell her that anyone can be sad at such a thing, and then move on to better thoughts. Not June. Something such as that builds in her. Perhaps she's misinterpreted the moment. Those people were, Sydney told her, happy. She said, "I saw them too. That's not sadness. It was hope. They were happy." But June's impression stays within June, inconsolable, irreconcilable and sharp.

"You make a trophy of it," Sydney said.

So when Bedri arrived at her doorstep she saw only the overgrown kid. Then his clothing askew, big smile, saying with exaggerated hand movements, *I am going with you, love/ I hope you remember the passports, red/ with our names / let us arrive, our arms genuine like guitars/ let us meet in frantic traffic/ let us meet in airports devastated with our love/ let us lie down together in pungent sheets.* He loved saying that last line, he and his seventeen-year-old friends broke out laughing at the delinquent and the erotic. Now. He was desperate and inaudible, the tears flooding his eyes, water running from his nose. A story about someone named Ghost and a Beemer.

❧

She wasn't judgmental, but Sydney was, obviously. And so, Sydney had retreated to her condo on the lakeshore and would probably not be heard from for days. But she knew Sydney wasn't vindictive, so she would not call the police.

"You always see things as political," Sydney had needled her.

"That's because they are."

"Sometimes things are just plain, June. You always have to find something that isn't there."

"And when did you gather these insights? Selling shit to people that they don't need!"

"As a matter of fact, yes. He's just a little thug, June. Not one of your . . . revolutionaries."

"You have absolutely no compassion, none. And for your information everything is political!" June was hissing.

"I know a little thug when I see one."

Sydney gave June a leather jacket for her birthday last year. June was appalled. The world Sydney lived in was full of "things" . . . leather jackets, shoes, flat-screened TVs, etcetera. June tried to appreciate the jacket but Sydney had seen the look on June's face. She didn't want "things," June said eventually. She told Sydney she wanted one embrace each day and one kindness each week. Sydney said, "Okay, that's easy. You're sure?" June said, "Yes, what I want is very simple."

But an embrace each day and a kindness each week can be very difficult. Nothing simple about it. Anyway, June found out Sydney could not do it. People can't be mindful constantly. Sydney started missing days, missing weeks and tried to make up again with "things." June of course was disappointed. She reasoned that perhaps, if someone could not give her an embrace a day or a kindness a week, perhaps there was something wrong with her. That Sydney couldn't do this made June sad. June thinks small things are deep and big things are shallow. So a little hole opened in her heart. She has a complicated system of feeling. She thinks if someone is so unaware of hurting someone, it stands to reason that if you tell them about it they'll be hurt themselves, since it will be a shock to them, they will crash when they understand how callous they've been. That would be a mountain of pain, June thinks, so she said nothing to Sydney, as she goes right on missing more and more days of embraces and more and more weeks of kindnesses.

No use going over that fight, June thought. She felt a small excitement. She could help Bedri, hide him, help him to leave town. It never occurred to her to tell him to go to the police himself. What good would that do? But regarding the thugs outside, in a minute she would open the front door and pretend to be dusting a mat. She folded her duvet, settling it beside the couch. She was wearing Sydney's shirt and a sleeping sarung. The Sri Lankan lover had given her one thousand sarungs, then he'd gone back to being a Tamil Tiger. Only last year she heard that he was in London giving someone else one thousand sarungs. He was writing a Sociology of Everything, and would send her e-mails on irrelevant matters concerning this every week. Each e-mail subject line ended with an exclamation point. Well, she had one thousand sarungs and if only for that he had not been a complete waste of time, they were a presence, an extravagant after-image of a fact. Love is love. It wears off. At the end there is a certain wonder at how you had become caught up in the domestic drama of it all—the immediate thrust and parry, the minutiae of emotional pain, plus a feeling as if you were once mad or as if you now need a transfusion of some kind of rare blood. At least she felt this way after each lover, needing some sort of rare blood to recover, as she first did when she was twenty, with the subway lover.

And that time with Beatriz. Beatriz sleeping was the rarest sight. June might have seen it only a few times.

Then the sheets were alive and secretive. A skin. Beatriz turned the sheets into skin. A thin translucent skin, some trembling substance June could touch but not enter. June wanted her to open the sheets and let her into what must be the incandescent atmosphere of this skin. So in those few moments when she came awake in the night, she wavered between watching the anomalous event of Beatriz sleeping and waking her with teeth in her back and rough hands tearing away the sheets' skin, between Beatriz's thighs.

To unravel that skin and to look at Beatriz, June was not quite sure what would happen. Would she catch her raw and even more dangerous, lethal perhaps? Beatriz did not look vulnerable in sleep like most people, she looked more of herself, more cool, more smoky, more clandestine as if she did not even allow her dreams to tell the truth. "I have held many people's lives in my hand," she told June. "I have held someone dying. Death is nothing and living is everything."

Sex with Beatriz was wordless and bruising. June felt every area of her body touched and scraped with Beatriz. Sydney talked throughout. June would stamp her lips or her fingers on Sydney's mouth in an unaccountable remembering of that brief time with Beatriz. She had returned to

Estelí. Was she killed by the Somocistas or was she now a bureaucrat, or a politician? Beatriz may not have even been her true name. When the Sandinistas won, June had searched the newspapers for the face of Beatriz riding into Managua in a jeep. She had not found her.

June chose dramatic lovers. Perhaps they expressed some drama going on inside her. It absorbed her how her lovers seemed to live in the world so immediately, as if all depended on the present moment that they were living. As if there was never a moment of contemplation needed. Meanwhile all she did was contemplate.

She opened the front door and shook the front mat just to let the dealer and his customers across the street know that they had been noticed. Perhaps that would make them move along. The windbreaker looked across at her, then went back to his business. She stared at him trying to cut his shiny, bubbled jacket in two with her look. Behind her she heard steps on the staircase. "Thanks, Miss June," she heard as Bedri rumpled past her going out the door. "Wait!" she managed to get out but he had run down the stairs and onto the pavement. She thought of calling him again as he hustled up the street but she didn't.

Emerging from the alley, the dealer and his clients had noticed the movement. Now they looked at her, lazily. She had pried into their private life, and now they were having a look at hers. Not interested enough to stay and judge, they hurried in the next direction themselves.

TWELVE

Bedri's knuckles were a faint violet. The veins of his eyes were violet too. He could smell violet when he pushed the door open and saw his sister.

His sister worked in a hair store. Whenever Bedri went to see her, he opened the door laughing and after that he could never get more than half of what he wanted from her. If only he could control his laughter, he knew, Hela would feel sorrier for him and give him what he asked of her, but he couldn't help himself. The hair store on Weston Road was tiny. Packets of hair in plastic wrap hung from the ceiling. The ceiling was so low in the store that the packets of hair hanging from it gave him the sense of being at a taxidermist's, though there were no bodies, no heads attached to the scalps. He couldn't help but laugh at the absurdity. His sister herself wore variations of these packets. Sometimes Hela wore Indian hair, sometimes Korean, sewing it into her scalp. Sometimes the hair was red, sometimes black. He asked her if she wasn't afraid of some disease or injury to her brain. He told her she would probably go bald if she wasn't careful.

This time he didn't laugh walking in. Hela was with a customer, a girl with long tiger-striped fingernails. He kept his violet bruised hand in his pocket, wiping his face with the other. He tried to act like a customer until his sister was finished and her customer left with three packets of hair. Hela picked up her purse and he wished that she hadn't. He read himself in that gesture. He usually came here for money, sometimes fighting her for it, grabbing her purse and running out. He saw their childhood and who he wished he had been to her, someone to count on instead of someone who always asked for money. He stood dejected.

Hela dug in her purse. She was grateful that he hadn't made a scene as he usually did, losing her a good sale. She brought out a small knot of money and simply held it out toward him, without blame, without love. She wanted him to leave quickly. He saw this. He wanted to stay. He wanted to have her want him to stay. He grabbed the money with his free hand failing and failing at finding a way to say, "Let me stay, Hela." No way he could say that in a pure unviolent way. A way without bruises. He left the store, stood outside for a few seconds looking at her through the glass front. She went back behind the counter. He saw relief on her face. She looked out, sensing she was being watched but he was gone. He was down the street near the traffic lights when he heard his name, his boy name, called—*Qualbiwanagoow! Goodhearted One!*—the name they all called him until he objected to it when he turned fourteen. The sound of it now filled him with hopefulness. And the sight of Hela waving him toward her made him run back like a boy, like a good-hearted one. She had heard him, she had heard him even if he hadn't said it. Let me stay, Hela. His injured hand bounced in his jacket pocket but the pain was nothing to him—his older sister was calling him back. When he got to her Hela said, "Don't go to Ma's work. She'll get fired if you do." She said it with venom, and thrust another knot of money toward him. He backed away from her and the money fell onto the pavement. She bent to pick it up and he turned and walked back from where he'd come. *Qualbiwanagoow! Goodhearted One!*

Qualbiwanagoow! Goodhearted One! He heard her calling him again but he didn't turn around.

His family was afraid of him, he thought, and that made him sad and desperate. He should go to Montreal with Ghost. He should disappear from them altogether. They would like that, he thought. His hand hurt again. Maybe it was broken. He pulled it out of his pocket. The violet had turned to blue. The second finger could not bend, the wrist, the whole hand was swollen. It hurt but it seemed to belong to someone else. The pain was big and dull and the more he looked at the hand the more foreign it seemed. He came to a bus stop and something made him hold his hand out for the people standing there to see. He reached the hand out to a girl with round white earphones. She didn't understand, brushed him away and turned back to her music. He paused, rebuffed, as if he had expected her to hold it. The two other people at the bus stop moved to a place away from him. He stood for a while, his hand still outstretched, then he turned and began running down the street with his hand extended.

He ran full out down Weston Road. He could hear a blue sizzling, a sound like twigs lit and crackling as he ran. He felt as if he was a fire burning through air. And he ran making sure the fire kept going until all the twigs were burned.

He didn't stop for the traffic light. He only saw his hand out in front of him, and then a school bus skittering alongside him seemed to disintegrate in speed. They were both speeding, he and the school bus, and now he felt like laughing. The school bus stopped but he didn't and he ran across the intersection at Jane without looking. It was a wide street. He ran over the middle verge and he noticed grass and a paper carton and then more asphalt. A red car went around his legs and a grey car rode on his left shoulder. The big lemon face of a semi-truck trailer came toward him and he dodged it and he heard a curse as if from underwater. A car drew alongside, blowing its horn. He followed his hand moving ahead of him. His feet were light and even in his heavy shoes he felt so very light. The Audi glided beside him like a small lake beside a highway. He felt like the highway, slender and fast. The horn from the Audi fluted. He heard shouting from a bird flying by, or a small plane. A plane, he decided, hovering to pick him up. He thought if he could get his hand up in the air he would be taken up, but he couldn't reach. He kept running and the lake beside him moved along with him. It was grey like an Audi, and rippling.

Weston Road wound its way before him and his legs began to melt. He thought they were burnt away and he felt sick to his stomach. He stopped and leaned over, vomiting.

The lake slowed beside him. He heard Ghost's voice saying something and he tried to put his hands to his ears.

"You're freaking out, man! You're tripping!"

Tripping, tripping, he heard, but he wasn't tripping, he was falling, he was tumbling in pain.

"Man up, Money."

He heard "man" and he straightened his upper body and ran at the Audi, kicking it.

"Blood! Blood! Blood, come! Let's go!" Ghost sounded wounded, beseeching, and Bedri opened the door and got into the lake. They sat in silence for a few minutes. The lake water lapped around them. Then Ghost said, "Let's roll man, let's roll."

"Whatever," Bedri said, not hearing himself say, "Whatever," but thinking he said, "Fuck, help!"

Ghost laughed and Bedri said, "What is so funny, I said help." And Ghost heard, "What the fuck you laughing at, I said roll."

All the way along Weston, they misheard each other that way. The car floated and Ghost put the music on, Bedri turned it off. They did this all afternoon. The car is a vault and they are locked in it with themselves and all the jewellery of their gloominess and their aimlessness. The steering wheel is gritty with sweat and dirt and the grist from their hands mixed with the grist of the guy he beat up—his mouth and face—all this damage is like gold dust to them. The CD player is playing Gnarls Barkley and they're singing the part about the echo and space.

On the back seat of the Audi now is Ghost's coat. There's no money in it, or not a lot. Lia had given him the coat and he thinks he'd better keep it because he'll probably never see his sister again. At least, not for a long time. In the trunk there's one side of a shoe that belongs to Ghost's mother. Ghost is keeping it. It's from Mercede's best pair and he took one side just to piss her off. It lies there like a bearer bond in the vault.

Bedri squeezes his eyes shut and open, he thinks they're swollen too. His hand is stiff and he pulls it from his coat pocket and notices that it is wrapped around the money Hela gave him. The money looks like newspaper or a subway transfer, or a receipt from a store and not at all like money. His coat is grungy and makes him hot and he gingerly takes it off, pulling the right sleeve gently over his wounded hand. He throws the coat in the back seat on top of Ghost's and notices a juice box, but then it looks like a brick and then like a metal bar. There's also a chocolate wrapper with a half eaten chocolate next to the metal bar, and there's a roach smoked halfway down. He sees a feather coming through the nylon threads of his jacket, a small grey feather and when he looks closer he thinks he can make out the bird it's attached to—a small grey bird. "There's a bird in the back seat," he says, picking up the roach and squeezing the lighter into the socket of the car. Ghost sucks his teeth, pulls out the lighter and passes it to him.

"You are soooo tripping, Money, where were you running to?"

Bedri lit and sucked on the roach. He knew the bird was there. He could see with the back of his head, the bird working its way out of the material of the jacket. He held his breath trying to make much of the residue of weed in the roach. The bird skitters out making a flittering sound, a sound with an "f" and a "z" in it. He passed the roach to Ghost who took it and sucked the rest of the residue out. "That's good," Ghost says from his clenched nostrils.

"Don't open the window, the bird will fly out," Bedri says. Ghost sputters out the thin smoke laughing. The bird z'ed and f'ed in the air of the back seat. It is loud even though Ghost doesn't hear it, but Bedri does. It's a small grey bird with a yellow triangular beak and blue feet.

It's still afternoon outside the car, the time of afternoon when schools are just out and kids are bumbling around on the pavements, running around each other with knapsacks on their backs. "Let's go," Bedri says, suddenly nostalgic with the scenes of shouting and running.

"Montreal?" Ghost asks.

"Yeah," Bedri says, "But don't open the window, the bird'll get out." Ghost is silent in case Bedri changes his mind. Then he says, "Wicked," and turns the car toward an artery of the city leading out.

"A brother is like one's shoulder," Bedri says and leans his heavy head on Ghost's shoulder. There is a momentary quiet. Even the bird went still. And the stillness is empty. Empty like something good. Like open time. Like if time opened an empty room. That's what Ghost is thinking. He would like to sit in an empty room and he would like his body to be scarless and he would like his mind to be empty with maybe a lake in it, a cool huge lake, one with small waves, way up north and far away from the city. Wasaga Beach where he went one time with Nonna and Nonno and Lia. Mercede was there too, he remembers. He walked very far out and the lake was still only at his small waist. He looked around himself and there was only water.

Bedri's heard this many times. *A brother is like one's own shoulder.* His father says it. His father wanted him to be more like his cousin, Ghedi, Khat-eater. Obedient. If he could he would, but he was never sure what his father meant by obedient. His father would make a series of grunts followed by a series of sayings that sounded like orders Bedri couldn't understand or carry out. Ghost understands him better than his father. He lifts his head, the Audi passes under a bridge, he opens his mouth to repeat his father's imprecations. *One cannot count on riches. A coward is full of precaution. He who does not shave you does not cut you.* They come to his head, his memory, but not to his mouth. His mouth remains open but quiet. The bird noise comes back. The bird wants to be let out, it flutters against the windows. He doesn't want it to hurt its wings. He opens his window, it beats against his eyebrow and flies off. Another bridge goes over the car. It looks to him as if the bird flew under it.

It is difficult to leave the city at certain times. The traffic hurrying out from three to eight p.m. is terrible, but the Audi will do its best, it will do all it can to take them where they want to go—Montreal, wherever. It heads for the highway.

THIRTEEN

There are twenty-four house sparrows living on a small shelf on the right side of June's house. In books, she has noticed these birds are mostly described as dun-coloured. She has watched them very closely. Small, quick birds, various declensions on brown and black and sand, flecks of red and even yellow, but if you were insensitive you would say dun. They are not ostentatious, these birds, but they have a nice sound. The new neighbours put up two bird feeders in their backyard and so, recklessly, according to June, increased the population of birds. Before that, there were nine house sparrows. She had made do with a cherry tree and a blackberry patch and a back and forth battle with the birds about the fruit. That was how it should be. A balancing act, not, in her opinion, an infantilizing of nature. She remarked to the neighbours that they were creating a false economy in the backyard. What would happen when they went away in the summers? What, when they forgot to replenish the bird feeders? This dependency they were encouraging was typical of liberals, she told them, it was maudlin and superior. Even the birds sensed the neighbours' insincerity, they did not nest in their walls but remained at June's. But having calculated the food supply as abundant, their rate of pregnancy had increased.

Actually, she thought, human beings operated in the reverse, decreasing as their well-being increases. Oh well, so much for drawing parallels. But each previous summer, she would find a dead baby bird or two tossed out of the nest. The house sparrows did not seem to tolerate any but the sturdiest and most aggressive babies. So that parallel might be true for human beings in the city: children seemed to be larger each year, puffed out on growth chemicals in processed food, and more callous and superficial too.

Hiking boots, socks, batteries, vitamin B ... June was making a mental list for the weekend camping in Algonquin Park, not something she liked to do, and did only because of Sydney. The neighbours' Jeep was idling in their garage at the back. June hated when they did that. Carbon monoxide. They were packing, she noticed, tent, chairs, canoe. She hoped they weren't going to the same place as she and Sydney. Then it struck her, who would feed their birds? She flew out to the backyard and shouted across the fence, "So, who is going to feed your birds while you are away?"

"We . . ." They both said "we" at the same time. They hadn't meant to answer her, let alone together. They were a couple and the man continued, "We left enough food." June hates the couple—heteronormativity was engraved on their foreheads.

"They are not pets. This is exactly what I warned you about."

"What?" the woman said.

"Eco-paternalism," June said, "You've created this bull- shit and now you're stepping away as if they're your pets and you're leaving them with the neighbour. With me."

"Look, June, give it a break," the woman yelled and went on packing the back of their Jeep.

The neighbours did not return for the next three weeks. The forlorn birds hung about surveying the bird feeders. June refused to lift a finger hoping the neighbours would never return so the world of the garden could find its balance again. But of course, she thought angrily, she now had to live with the knowledge of the situation all around her. The neighbours had upset the ecological balance and now famine would occur. They had changed the tastes of the sparrows, substituted some industrial chemical diet for the natural one, purely, on their whimsy. They fed the sparrows on whimsy. *Whimsy, whimsy, whimsy,* June repeated to herself. This for June was the worst kind of selfishness and superiority disguised as empathy.

June disliked starlings. They sought each day to displace the sparrows. She did not like their twitter or their sharp yellow predatory beaks. And she had no appreciation for their multi-coloured glistening feathers, at once green, blue, red, gold and black. She understood they lived in a communal nest that could take over an attic. This would otherwise be admirable to her as the phenomenology of socialism but she hated the aggression of starlings. If the neighbours decimated the sparrows with their goodwill and their fast-food bird feed, June knew the starlings would move in. One act always sets a whole array of acts in motion. In retrospect what begins innocently enough, without thought, compels a certain disaster.

A misanthrope, though she thought of herself in quite opposite terms. She found most people cruel despite their stated intentions; most people in the city thrashed about getting this and that without thinking of the consequences, she believed, even though most of them thought they were good people. Like starlings. More and more now, over this summer, the sound of sparrows would be replaced by the sound of starlings. This is in the summer of course. One thing the winter can be counted on for is stasis. Lovely stasis.

Sydney was June's first lover without a cause. No political talk except June's, no meetings except June's, nor urgent phone calls except June's.

Nothing like Beatriz all those years ago. Though there was never any question of Beatriz being permanent. Beatriz could not bear the English language, and her whole life was waiting for her in Estelí. But had there been a question, let us say there was a chance she might have stayed longer, it would have been nuclear between them. In the short months of Beatriz's appearance in the city, only her life, with its secrets, mattered. She whispered gutturally into

telephones, she checked hidden notes, she made calcula-
tions and her whole body was like a bit of reddened coal.
At the time June did not expect more than that; Beatriz was
clearly passing through and this explosive impermanence
was precisely what June wanted at the time. Not love but
the fissive encounter, the intense ideas and intense sex and
the hypersense that every moment was atomic and defining.
Of course one cannot live at that pitch forever, though
naturally one wants to.

Sydney was a breath of fresh air. *Something to be said for that
cliché,* June said aloud. Sydney went to work in the mornings, did the minimum at a consumer retail clearing
company, knowing reflexively, instinctively—whereas June
only knew it analytically—that the working class was
exploited and she should not do too much to increase the
wealth of the corporate class. Sydney could not wait to get
out of work, get back on Highway 400 and call June to
start up their real life every evening. Life began for Sydney
after five, and that meant dinner and movies and wine and
dancing on Fridays and Saturdays, and sex without fail all
day Sunday, and anytime in between, including just before
work in the mornings. Especially before work in the mornings, because how else to pass the day talking on the phone
trying to sell useless things to people who wanted to buy

useless things, like satellite radios, for listening to the use-less radio playing, over and over again, useless songs. Sydney took the boredom of selling for granted.

June thought there was a rich vein of innocent ore running through Sydney's mind. That's what she called it, a rich vein of innocent ore. Meaning that there was a spontaneous space in Sydney that had not yet been dragged down by the world, neither June's world nor the world at large. Sydney seemed always uplifted—albeit by gadgets and shoes and designer dark glasses and new cars and new watches. Not dogmatic like June. Every dinner together was therefore loaded with June's sense of history, June's theories on social economy. She deconstructed where the meat came from and where the asparagus. "So that's why it tastes so good!" Sydney would mock, biting down on a breast of chicken. "Just be thankful, June." June would be slightly chastened and shut up. Only slightly. She didn't want to spoil Sydney. Spoil all that zeal for life. She had a feeling that she could. She was smarter, she thought, and so more brutal than Sydney. Like a starling.

Truly, June was afraid. What should be intensifying in her was waning. She had had no particular landing spot in mind yet the Women's History Archive was not where she thought she would end up. Her reticence had settled her there. She was afraid that all the grasp of the worldly, all the passion was leaving her. And so she was hanging on to Sydney for much more than she was willing to admit. Yes, she was more brutal. The kind of brutality that comes as it had come to her father, how to put it, with clarity. "I see the fucking world clearly, Sydney. You don't. We are just hanging on a ball of hard mud spinning in space at a ridiculous speed. That's us, that's the earth. A ball of mud, hanging and hurtling nowhere."

"Can I drink my wine in peace? Because if it's like that then it doesn't matter, and I should have a little more wine to enjoy the muddy ride."

"It's a muddy ride all right. Drink your wine and be unaware ..."

"But if I'm aware, what good is it? You said yourself ..."

"I just thought that meanwhile, while we are clinging to this ball of mud, the very least we could do is ... is ..."

June doesn't want to change anyone, she doesn't want to knock anyone off their axis. At least, not in relation to her. She wants Sydney to come to understand without her persuasion. Then again, June doesn't know if she's being coy or calculating or if she's being principled. So anyway, silence is the best thing. This silence is the short path from free love to love. As soon as this silence comes between them June begins to want more than she's wanted. And since silence is so big, what she wants fills it to a far larger extent than she anticipates. If she'd said anything like, "Sydney, you are not giving me what I asked for and what you promised," perhaps Sydney would have understood and straightened up. Sydney had no idea that the lapse, regarding the embraces, was so important. But June continued to say nothing and to let her resentment and disappointment fill an ever-expanding rift. Sydney remained chipper and cheery as ever, full of talk about people at the office, the people on the street; bringing bootleg videos, buying more shoes and gloves, more electronics. The house is filling up with crap as far as June is concerned but it is completely empty of what June wants—one embrace a day, one kindness a week. As long as Sydney's there though, June thinks there's that possibility down the road. But she could not help but grow slightly bitter at the fact that this is a small thing she's asked, such a small thing. Sydney would never understand if June didn't pay special attention to Sydney's birthday, as a case in point. Birthdays were an elaborate event where "things" were acquired, soon to be discarded. June hated Sydney's birthdays. Especially after the embraces, and kindnesses she herself asked for, were not given. But June doesn't like to dwell because once an idea is in her head it bounces and bounces like a pendulum and never goes away.

Existence is futility and smallness, June thought. Then looking at Sydney she reversed herself. Because if she, June, was right, then truly there was no hope. But if Sydney was right, even if Sydney didn't understand, intrinsically, where or why there was hope, then it existed. She could not always abide Sydney's optimism—which wasn't really optimism, she thought, but consumerism. Sydney acted as if you had to attack each day with all your desires, your retail desires. She herself had big desires, she thought. Big, and high-minded. She'd been, as she said to Sydney on various occasions, in the trenches. "You wouldn't know Sydney. You just wouldn't."

Sydney tolerated June's superiority, primarily because she didn't respect it. She measured everything like this: first, June was poor so where did she get off being superior? Second, Sydney liked university women, women who talked intellectual talk and acted superior, especially in public. Though in private Sydney would say, "Can you get to the point quickly? Why do you always have to lengthen out a story?" And June would say, "That's the point of a story, Sydney. If you don't know the ins and outs, the details, what is the point of the conclusion?"

"The point is the end," Sydney said, "You take so long and you think what you're saying is so interesting and you lose the thread."

"Those are called digressions," June said.

Third, Sydney's attraction to June was ultimately carnal. She found June's distraction and inattention carnal. June did not know that she was sensual. When she went on her rants she appeared sexually suggestive to Sydney, her political intensity physical.

"Digressions?" Sydney said, "Let's say you have a lot of digressions. And I want the conclusion."

Unconscious. That is what June thinks of Sydney. But she wishes she were like Sydney, able to place such moments in perspective or, better still, *not* see them at all. How many of these gestures she had kept in her—the family at the store window; the little girl passing a hand over her face like a worried old lady at a corner; the thin wrist of a girl in her mother's hand, a teenaged boy on a wide city street that opened like a grisly maw to his future. Precariousness, everywhere June saw precariousness. That's a gift she'd like to give back.

Once, in Accra, among the vendors passing at the vehicle window with water, nuts, toys for sale, she saw a woman begging with her family. There were two boys, two girls and the mother. June was in a Jeep with friends from Kumasi. She'd met them casually in Lomé, and since they were driving west from Togo to Kumasi in Ghana she took a ride with them. Kumasi had been a major centre of the slave trade and June was on the great return—backpacking and hitching where she could. She would not do that today—those were the days when you could wander the world without encountering geopolitical violence everywhere. But even then, there had been an attempted coup right after she left Ghana in 1979. There was always the regular violence of rape, of course, no matter where, like a time on the subway in Mexico City in 1973 and that close call in this city when she left her second-floor window open. Violence is regular, June thinks, in general, regular. In Accra a family had come up to the Jeep's windows and begged for money, putting their hands to their mouths to gesture that they were hungry. They were in a battle against each other as much as for each other. The friends from Kumasi ignored the family but June opened the window and put one cedi out the opening. A girl snatched it and began running and the other children took off after her. The mother kept putting her hand to her mouth and tapping at the window. The van moved off and June looked back, which was June's fate, looking back and seeing sorrow.

Sydney would see this family as surviving, striving on the streets of Accra.

Even in sleep this faculty doesn't abate. The time June was in a plane crash in the Comoros Islands, it actually happened in a dream. She was flying to god knows where in that plane. It had left Tanzania and was banking east towards Madagascar. The sky bent like blue aluminum on a dented roof and June reached her hand out the window to smooth it out. The other passengers were watchful, hoping that June would manage to even out the atmosphere to the east long enough to get to Madagascar. June held the long blue plate of the heavens, her fingers stroking the corrugated air. But then someone said, "What are you doing?" and June turned to answer that she was doing what she had been asked, and the metal roof of the world fell onto the plane. The plane had the skin of a whale's body and June saw its grey blood leak through a window. The next morning the radio said there had been a plane crash in the Comoros and June woke up with one side of her body bruised blue and her left eye bloodshot.

FOURTEEN

If you were to notice every small physical gesture of an individual person and if you observed those small gestures over the course of a year and a half, say, and if you were to lose that person you should be able to find that person. Like tracking the genome sequence, but the genome sequence of gestures. You should be able to find that person. You should.

Lia sees Jasmeet everywhere. In glimpses and sketches she finds her chromosomes. Jasmeet's arm. There it is in an older woman's arm, the wrist mainly. Jasmeet's left foot there, in a man's foot resting on a concrete plant box on University

Avenue. Jasmeet's eyebrows, there, in the plucked eyebrows of a waitress at the Renaissance Bar. People disappear all the time, but Lia is sure that Jasmeet has returned and simply does not want to be found. That is, Lia cannot gather all her genetic observations into one solid body. That is all.

The city is approaching daylight again as Lia looks at the lake out her new window. It would be great to live here, they had both agreed, so close to the city but so separated from it by this strip of the great lake. And just so Jasmeet knows, wherever she may be collecting herself, she's done it, she's moved to the island. How come we don't collect beauty in the brain? Lia thinks. It doesn't seem collectable. It's fleeting. People can collect paintings, they can collect objects that may be beautiful, but this is not the same as collecting beauty. Collecting beauty would be remembering exactly, immersing yourself in the exact moment of an image or an act, and storing it in some synaptic folder in the brain to be called upon with the same effect as one recalls pain, for example. Pain collects itself like its own curator. Pain is so uncalled, so unsummoned. Beauty should have the same capacity. But it doesn't and Lia knows why. She's figured it out, beauty doesn't damage. It doesn't burn a hole right through you, an unfillable hole. It doesn't incinerate you. It does not damage.

The window that Lia is staring out of, thinking this thought—that beauty doesn't damage—opens to the lake. She's found a new room on Ward's Island, just a short ferry ride away from the city. It is a room on the top floor of a small two-storey clapboard house and a painter with two dogs lives downstairs. The house gives her a new vantage point on the city. When she rides the ferry to this house on Ward's Island there is a sense of pulling away; of leaving Toronto without leaving it, and of seeing the receding city whole, lined along the lake, the valleys of houses, the mountains of glass towers. Out of her top floor window now, streaks of light grey are appearing in a blue-grey sky; soon those will be followed by a pale orange hue. All these minute light changes she wants to collect. She likes waking at this hour. It's a new thrill for her. So much goes on before the distant city fully comes awake. At first the city is misty, then phosphorescent, then it emerges skyscraping, glittering, a muted noise crossing the lake toward her.

No place she had ever lived with Mercede ever saw these blues, or ever observed the increments of beauty seen from this window. Up at five every day, TV packaging plant at eight, home at seven. Now nineteen she had never had regularity, routine, sameness. That's what she'd needed most of all, a life without jagged peaks, a life she could make all on her own. And when Jasmeet befriended her and invited her to her shows, her parties, her chatty philosophies, Lia tentatively, and then with something like joy, felt she had fully entered her new life. She'd found herself confiding in Jasmeet. Telling her about her mother, Mercede, about her brother, Germain, about Nonna and Nonno. Confiding so much it came as a shock and an insult when Jasmeet called Mercede an emergency. Indiscreet, that is what she had felt, indiscreet and disloyal. She's not ready for friendships, she concludes. She doesn't know how they work.

Here, she spends the first wakeful hour of the day collecting these slivers of light, of tree, of water. She has a notebook. She's drawn columns in it and here, on weekends especially she makes notes as to each incremental change of the day. She's running out of names for blue and grey and green. Blue marrow, blue positions, blue speed, she's written, grey snare, grey freeze, grey grain. Green terminal, green engines. She ought to buy a camera, then she could set it at the window and take shots each minute. But then again, that would not quite do for what she needs. The camera would take the picture but she needs the moment to sink into her, to somehow become chemical, to metabolise, to reconstitute, yes, reconstitute her heart.

When she looks back at her daily jottings, she realises

it's not recordable in words. She wants a more porous surface, where beauty can come into her, metamorphose, suffuse her skin. She sits still for that first hour of the day but old anxieties erupt, like how is Mercede, where is Germain, where is your ghost? Phantom emergencies course through her blood. She misses the 6:45 ferry, takes the next dragging Jasmeet's bike on; when the ferry docks on the city side, she rides west along the lake's shore and then north up the main artery of Bay Street toward the city's centre. Her nonna's language and Mercede and Germain trail along beside her.

The main corner at Bay and Bloor is jammed when Lia gets there. Corporate ads have overrun all surfaces, static here, moving there. The sidewalks are bursting. It's her first season, the sweet season of summer. Everyone on the street is late for something. When you're late you either feel panic or freedom. Perhaps you missed an appointment or a deadline; you were supposed to have stepped over some threshold, entered some doorway, sat down in some cubicle with a smile. So now everyone on the intersection is between these fates. Panic or freedom amounts to the same thing if you look at it right. When you're late you've missed a moment and therefore all the others that would have followed. There's a slight regret because back in the life you had, the life heading toward the threshold, the doorway, the cubicle, you thought it was important to cross that threshold, that doorway, or to sit down in that cubicle at this certain time. But you're late, so that's over. Lia watches all the latecomers confront this moment as she does too. She should park the bike at the Bay Street subway and take the train west to Kipling. Flat-screen televisions wait on the line to be packaged and sent out.

A young woman beams from the crowd at the crosswalk and she's got an in-between face: she isn't sure whether to be alarmed or satisfied. To be lost or to be free. She was intending to be sensational showing up at work today. She's wearing white stretch jeans, a tank top and a boa. Maybe she wanted to be fired, she looks like Saturday night on Richmond Street. She was looking forward to the celebrity of stepping off the elevator as if stepping out of a club, and maybe she still can. She's late, definitely, with nothing to lose now. She glimpses Lia on the bike staring at her and determines to go up to the 19th floor anyway where she answers phones in a law firm. Who is the biker with the baggy pants to tell her what to do? She's misinterpreted Lia of course.

The young woman in the boa will either go up to the 19th floor or she won't.

"Good luck!" Lia yells at the young woman as she locks Jasmeet's bike to a meter near the subway.

"Thanks!" the woman in the boa yells back at her. And there's their laughter ricocheting in the black diamonds of the intersection. The woman lifts the boa like a flag crossing the street toward the office block. She enters the elevator and is beamed to the 19th floor. She thinks of it as being beamed. She appears on the threshold of McArthur and Elliot, LLP, like a star. She turns her face up as if the fluorescent light is a camera that loves her and she lasts until the first coffee break when her supervisor asks her for a private word. She packs up the few mementos on her desk, a signed photo of Usher, a Rubik's Cube and a coffee mug with the declaration "This Sucks!" and she leaves. The supervisor is waiting, ready with a speech about proper attire and punctuality, a speech with a heavy shovel of morality and paternalism. He likes her, wants her to make progress in the firm. That is what he likes to think, though there's no progress for a receptionist except perhaps to drinks with the partners, barbecues in the summers or illicit not-to-be-spoken-of late intimacies in the firm's leather chairs. All this passes through the supervisor's thoughts until he realises she is late again, late for their tête-à-tête and he calls the front desk. There's no answer and he leaves his office to check on her only to see the elevator doors close and someone incandescent descending. When the building's doors let her out she is at another intersection altogether. Transposed. She could do anything now, learn to dance, learn an instrument, study anthropology. She wants to do something that doesn't involve other people lording over her. She's had enough of the weight of lawyers, the weight of real-estate brokers and the weight of coffee buyers. It's all weight. Each day she would go to the job and every-one would sit on her chest and her pelvis. *Weight, weight, weight.* That's why she wore the boa this morning, for flight. Her mother and father of course would not get this. They are used to weight, they think weight is nor-mal. They don't mind the house getting heavier and heavier with the weight she brought home added to the weight they brought home. Oh no. They thought all this weight means she is growing up. Well, they would have enough to say when she told them that she would no longer be bringing any weight home.

Apparently you can weigh a thought, and different thoughts have different weights. Beauty is not weight. That is why it doesn't stay long, that is why it doesn't damage. The weight of beauty is negligible. Lia would like to be damaged by beauty. Wouldn't we all? You forget it so quickly. If only it could accumulate. If only it could pile up. Like, for instance, gathering together all the mornings when you wake up with not a care, not a worry. Perhaps beauty could adhere to the skin, be like sweat or hair. Over on the island Lia feels untethered. As if she's connected to no one, and disconnected from everyone. She is only intent on this one thing now: beauty. And why? Because, it weighs less than pain. She's seen it through a window, it is a combination of light and time, a random combination of light and time and matter.

Last night for instance Lia went foraging on the internet and found *Asterope markii*. This butterfly is indescribable. Black-blue, Dotted Glory, spotted on the left lower quadrant then its basal side is bright orange and red. What accounts for that in a butterfly? Then she saw *Asterope* pinned, spread-eagled on eBay for $3.99 each. She would have liked to buy one but, her hand hovering over the cursor, she thought better of it. That *Asterope* would not be sitting still on the edge of the Amazon forest, its appearance quiet and surprising.

Like the appearance of a certain thought. Did Mercede ever love her? And Germain. Her ghost. Or her nonno. Nonna? Had anyone ever loved her? Descending into the subway she is heavy with this thought. She's blown away by the thought: none of them. Wow. *Wow, wow, wow.* How careless. How careless they all are. And now, if she could unhook herself from them all. She thinks of a bat now, *Balionycteris maculata*, unhooking itself from its membrane. It is the smallest fruit bat in the world, she recalls again from last night's foraging for beauty. She looks for its spots on her hands. Spotted-winged, it's called. Its spots, fluorescent, marking its joints. This bat is perfect, and has thought of everything, including the day it will unhook itself from its membrane. It has marked its joints in case it forgets. And in the meantime that fluorescence is a warning to predators, she imagines, and a sign to family. The westbound train to Kipling glares through the tunnel. She will try to live as perfectly as this bat.

FIFTEEN

Ghost and Bedri loop into the city again. They are aimless, indecisive, and the city is like the cardinal home of a boomerang. They can't get adrift of the place.

"Gravity bends time," Ghost says.

"A madman does not lack wisdom." Bedri giggles.

"I know shit people don't even think I know." Ghost laughs. "If we slingshot back into town it'll be a different day and a different time."

"A difficult day?" Bedri mishears.

"A *different* day," Ghost corrects. He is always having to correct. Correct Bedri, correct Mercede. Correct the guy sitting in the Beemer. *Correct, correct, correct.* But he was not always certain that he was right and sometimes in the middle of him there is a hole.

"A different day," Bedri nods. "A different day. I'm down with that. A person stands next to shade, not next to words." Bedri's hand is throbbing beyond pain. It will always throb. It will always feel as if it is melting; as if some fire ate it.

"Yep," Ghost agrees, "you're a fucking philosopher, man."

"Like how . . . like if you come down in the right place."

"Yeah, like we don't see it right, but the earth right, has big bumps and then massive ditches where gravity is stronger. If we find the ditch . . ."

"We could go anywhere?"

"Anywhere."

"Okay," Bedri says. "Let's do that."

The car speeds up, Ghost's foot hammering the gas pedal. He presses hard trying to turn gas into nuclear accelerant. If he could go fast enough they could ricochet down the Don Valley Parkway towards the lake. Maybe they would arrive in the city in another time.

They had no place to go, really. There was the imaginary idea of Montreal, there was the nothing time in their heads, the time when and where they would have what they thought of as a life. Time hanging out, leaning against cars, smoking or drinking. Their clothes would be fine, maybe they'd be barebacked with six pack stomachs and gunning arms, maybe those arms would be wrapped around a girl who had long bare legs. Maybe they would lift those girls in the air with one hand.

The Audi was a dream box, and they both had the same dream. As long as the car kept running nothing would happen that was important or connected to anything outside of it. Ghost's right hand clasped the gearshift. He was in *Contact* like Jodie Foster, going faster and faster, creating a black hole to shift time, to catch up with time and to go past time. Like their bodies were electrodes, or sound waves melded to the body of the Audi. Down in the city the lights were out. They heard a great pop when the Audi leapt and the city fell into darkness. Everything could suddenly be heard without engines and electricity. A child said, "Where's Papa?" Then a woman said, "He's down the road." But the child said again, "Where's Papa?" And a dog barked and airplanes tried to lift off, but all that could be done was grass growing at a terrible speed and all that could be heard was a long quiet.

The Audi is shaping into a nuclear cylinder and Ghost waxes about shit he knows for certain. "Energy is mass times speed and at the speed of light mass and energy are like the same ... and speed is distance divided by time. At the speed of light you can bend time ... like make a black hole ... if we drive at the speed of light ..." It is perfect, Bedri thought. His hand is almost perfect in this time. The Audi digests this theory, the elegance of it. It takes 100,000 years to cross the galaxy at the speed of light, but waves, invisible events, violent waves hit all the time. Like Bedri's fist, for example. Gravitational waves hit the earth, we only need the smallest change.

"Perfect, Blood," Bedri agrees. It was like what happened to his hand and his coat. The bird flying out of it. Maybe the hand would subside if they could do this; if they could arrive on a different day. His perfect day would be what he wondered. Yeah, music would be in it for sure and a girl with a voice like Angie Stone.

"Angie Stone?"

"Yeah, Angie Stone, what's wrong with that, Blood?"

"Old school man, Rihanna."

"I don't care. Angie Stone is mine."

Anyway, they'd be at a club, like the Guvernment, and they'd just be cool. It would be summer and they'd walk across the street to the lake and just sit there. But the day would start clear and sunny and he'd look out his window first and feel good. And there'd be no father coming home to darken the living room. He would get breakfast and play music and dance. And then he would shower and put on some clothes and call his girl with the voice like Angie Stone and they would spend the whole day cruising and stopping to have sex wherever they wanted.

"What's wrong with that?"

"Nothing man, nothing. That's my perfect day too. She'd be a freak though, my girl Rihanna. Like that."

"No more fuckups."

"No more dickheads."

Anyone would want a day like that. Simple. The problem was gravity and the answer was gravity. Gravity held this simple possibility, it held them both to the time they were in and it could unleash them from time.

"We have the car."

"Yeah, we can do this."

"Anything. We can do anything, fuck it."

The Audi sped up, it shone like a new skin, a glistening meteor skin. It cut in and out of slower sluggish cars. It spun into the southbound Don Valley Parkway heading for the waiting city.

SIXTEEN

If June had the chance to be born again she would prefer to be born in the countryside. There you notice how life is, however brutish it may be. Animals eat animals, grass dies away and springs back, some insects flourish one year then fail another, and that's the way life is. But nothing one sees in the city truly instructs one as to the course of events; as to the flow of life and death in the natural world. One expects immortality in a city and that is delusional. And if someone were to say that indeed the city is not the natural world, June would say death is when we enter the natural world no matter how cunning the artifice of the

city. In the city death is abrupt; unexpected and unfortunate, most of all unfortunate. No one expects it and it is
always taken as a tragedy. As if the joys of the city are so
great and the juice of living there so sweet. In a city, it is
as if you will miss some great moment if you die. In the
countryside death is ragged and random, it doesn't seem
as selective and vindictive as in the city. June thinks it's
because everyone in a city thinks they're so special. They
think that they get a special visit from mayhem when in
fact mayhem is normal in the world. The city tries to keep
out randomness and mayhem, it is in a prolonged and constant battle with these two concepts. June observes the
waste water of these two elements every time she steps
outside. That is why she would rather have been born in
the countryside.

More spacious, more organic, she thinks, sitting at Tim
Horton's. Sibyl might pass by. Bedri might pass by. It could
have been random—his finding her and telling her the
story, like a kindergarten boy running in and gushing out a
set of words then rushing out again. He's disappeared into
the elements of mayhem and randomness. They are indeed
elements, June thinks, like iron or mercury. Of course June
knows she's being a little precious. She laughs at herself out
loud. Right now she is probably an odd-looking woman in

the coffee shop. She looks around and laughs again. Everybody in the coffee shop is odd-looking except those who have someone sitting across from them talking. Companionship makes you look sane. There could be two perfectly crazy people sitting together but that act of social mingling legitimises their sanity. Ridiculous, June thinks. This is another act of cultivation, of keeping out the mayhem. She will probably never hear from Bedri again. There are, these days, so many newspaper articles about him, or someone like him.

It's not entirely impossible to make out what's what in this city. The people underneath are living, muddling through. The people on top keep the people below in their sights. Predators are always aware of their prey. That's what June thinks. This was the fatal lesson her father had learned. He had died of alcoholism. June didn't go to the funeral. It was a long time ago in another country. Her mother had survived him and actually thrived on his insurance policy, living in a condo in Florida. At the beginning of his last illness her father had made lengthy, almost exuberant, notes on local entities, political and corporate, detailing accusations of undermined democracy, government collusion with oil companies and widespread graft. He said these mechanisms owed him for the wastage of his life. June received six red ledgers in a parcel from her mother, a parcel also containing a rich black Christmas cake. A paradox. She imagines her mother laughing from Florida.

She thinks of herself as always alert though she is always taken a little off guard. Sibyl's gone missing. Bedri's gone missing. And sometimes she falls into a sentimentality, a stasis. She was aware that her view was dim then. Her mother had said as much on the phone when telling her of her father's death. "You go about your business dear, don't mourn, don't worry with your father. He is in a better place." June had kept silent on her end of the line. Was her mother being sarcastic? Then her mother said in a conspiratorial voice, "He thought too much about the world. You watch yourself. Don't care so much about the world. He was too much in it. I would be dead myself if I thought like that."

One thing must be said, June loved a good sunset. Once, there was a sunset so orange, due to pollution of course, but so orange the buildings were set on fire simply through the heat that the colour orange makes. June could swear the back wall of the house where she lived was singed with that sunset's glow. She ran outside in case the house lit on fire. She saw the hot dye of the ending sun fill in the sky where the houses had left spaces. And once she saw a full moon hang on the summit of a skyscraper. She called Sydney to say, "Go outside now and look at that." To see an almost non-obscured sunset in the city you have to go down to the lake, otherwise sunrise or sunset are concepts. Inferences. You imagine them and infer that they exist because there's light and dark in the world or in any day. Light approaches or recedes, darkness approaches or recedes, that's how you know.

Trevor, still dancing in the photograph with her, is dead now. June used to hear from him now and again after he left for New York. In those phone calls she always imagined his delightful smile when he said, "Oh my god, New York is wicked!" but his calls petered out and years went by without a sign of him. Then one summer walking by the lake June met one of the other dancers and she asked, "Have you heard from Trevor?" The other dancer looked incredulous, "Trevor died four years ago," she said. June felt faint, she fell. "You didn't know?" the dancer asked, holding June's hands. "How could he die?" June sent these words out as if they were four last breaths. "He died in a small room in New York," the dancer said, "Alone and sick." The day ended right there for June. More streets disappeared from the grid of the city, more oxygen was burned away.

SEVENTEEN

Time is turmoil. Cutting down the belly of the city, the Don Valley Parkway is a sticky bituminous river; its narrow, slick lanes are carnivorous. It is possible that what follows is a probable future. Every day is changeable. The Audi is a silverfish, a mechanical violent silverfish, nocturnal, wingless, boring down the Don Valley. It becomes exoatmospheric, it gains flight. And the two young men dream into the lives they want. However provisional, however small, however impossible we might think their dreams are. Who wants to live in the lives they have in the present? A lot of dreams get shanked because of money. Or gas. Or the absence of a vision. So? They arrive now on their own adrenaline and they are the romantic young men they want to be. They are coiled and muscled and elegant and they have girls on their shoulders. Their hearts are calm. All the carbon monoxide gushed out and oxygen filled the vacuum. The car leapt a few possible worlds. They breathe some bristling shiny element, they fill their lungs full of it.

Bedri wears glasses here. He wears glasses because of the wheat of pure light they passed through—he had kept his eyes open so he could be wounded. He holds that hand, the one that did all that damage that he can't remember anymore, he holds it like a jewel, he holds it like it's a thing he should know the value of, it is still a little brittle, its bones are porous, and it can't take too much cold or too much heat. But he reckons that's the least that could have happened and that's penance and mercy. He fixes computers. They both do, he and Ghost. They work on making things run faster, on diagnosing what makes systems slow down.

Ghost has a baby here. The first thing he did when they arrived in lustrous metal was make a baby. He closed his eyes, gravity bent time and his heart fell open like a cave. And he carries the baby everywhere with him even on his bike when he goes around the city looking for his mother and his sister, Lia. She was the smart one, and he hopes to find her, his ghost one day, to do something simple with her, something airy, perhaps have a coffee. He wants to tell her of his gravitational theory and how it worked, or perhaps he simply wants to tell her he's fine and everything is okay, he has a baby, he has a life. And astonished, she'll say to him, *"Germain! What the hell!"* When they're at home the baby crawls onto him and plays with the scar on his chest and he feels as if the baby's hand is sinking past the scar and into his heart. The baby's happy at the back of the bicycle. The baby loves the back of the man whose back is like a railing and the baby thinks of it as a railing and reaches for the man all the time. Ghost leans back the way a railing should lean back and he feels the small hands of the baby and he giggles and the baby giggles.

The Don Valley Parkway swallows sound, it crushes time.

Nothing is inevitable. Mornings perhaps, evenings. Those are not in our control, but you can't be sure of anything else. Not even disaster. If you look at a sky in the city it seems inconsequential until you really look at the sky. Like this August, to the west it is blue and pinkish orange, it seems to have its own thoughts and its own existence, its own plans.

EIGHTEEN

Sydney struggles up from sleep. The radio alarm has gone off for the third time and the drive north out of the city to Barrie is cruel and relentless. As taut as a garot. She isn't looking forward to it. There is the smell of scotch from the glass beside the bed. Last night Sydney loved drinking scotch from the deep gorge of June's back. Laphroaig. It was a good morning now that Sydney remembers last night, or had it been two a.m.? June is sometimeish. She likes having scotch drunk from her body at odd times. Likes the coolness, the lethal feel of Sydney's teeth on her back, Sydney's tongue on her waist where the scotch ran off her onto the bed; Sydney biting her hip and her thigh.

Sydney smells smoke but thinks it is a dream or perhaps the neighbours. June doesn't smoke and the walls between them and the neighbours are porous. She gropes for the side of the bed, situates the path to the bathroom. June is standing by the window. She is smoking. "Why are you smoking?" Sydney says, rolling out of the bed, heading to the bathroom. "No, never mind. I don't have time, but why are you smoking? You don't smoke."

"I do now, what the fuck," June says. Sydney makes this mistake each morning, asking June a question just as the highway looms. Why not save these questions for later? Sydney makes it to the shower. June follows her, leans in through the doorway, then sits on the toilet smoking. "They're saying they will do a thorough environmental assessment," she starts laughing then coughing, "A thorough assessment."

"And?" Sydney is trying to enjoy the heat of the shower and lets it run silently for a few more minutes before shutting it off.

"Such liars. If they ever, ever truly did a 'thorough' environmental assessment of anything they would have shut all this shit down long ago. We're talking about a pipeline, Sydney, running through water tables and food lands. The gut of the continent. Sydney, do you want your hot shower and your car so bloody much that we have to destroy the world?"

"Well I don't want to go foraging for wood at this hour, and I can't walk a hundred kilometres." Sydney does not want to have to form these words or any words. The shower has made her bright. The two a.m. Laphroaig has washed away.

"Fine." June gets up, throws the cigarette into the toilet bowl where it sizzles. "Don't think about it."

"I'm not." Sydney rummages around in the closet. "I can't do anything about it and I don't want to think about what I can't do anything about." She is looking for panties, the black ones, the Jockeys.

"Fine, don't think about it."

"I don't intend to." And Sydney pauses in realisation, before, "Ah, you haven't heard from that kid, have you?"

June is quiet. Sydney doesn't like that sound. It is the precursor of unbearable mornings in June's bedroom and this morning is unbearable so quickly.

"You always pick a fight after good sex," Sydney says, quite naked, "Do you know that? You always pick a fight. You have to spoil it."

June is brought up short, a little less certain, taking in Sydney's point. "I do not."

"Well, fight by yourself this morning," Sydney marches out to the hallway, slamming the bedroom door.

She does *not* fight after good sex. Sydney simply *cannot* handle a serious discussion, Sydney did not have enough sophistication or interest and in the mornings June needs a bracing appraisal of the world to open her day. Well, clearly she can be gloomy at times, she does admit. That is why she needs someone who can take up the argument with enthusiasm and help her to clarify the meaning of the world. Not someone who wants to act as if the world were not about anything serious. One simply has to be aware of global warming, eco-justice, geopolitical strategies, in June's book, to get up in the morning with any sense of human events. What kind of brain, June wonders, would wake up to an alarm clock with not a clue about what is happening and only the thought of what is for breakfast, or lunch, but utterly dismissive of the great moments of human history?

She wishes it were easy. Food, drink, sex. These, as pleasures, happened to her in some mechanical structure of her brain but the main engine ran on what was wrong with the world. When did that engine start spewing the greasy film of what was wrong? The year she got her glasses, perhaps fourteen. The year she solidified a desire to know every detail of conditions in the world. That way she could see the angles and not act without thought. And why would it have occurred to her at fourteen? Fourteen is precisely the age to act without thought. But if you walk down a street and find a parallel version of your life, then you must become aware of the world and being aware of it means you can do something about it. You have a chance.

Sydney, returning, says to June, "You know, June, you think love is complicated but it's very simple."

"Love is simple? Are you joking? Then why is it love? And who was talking about love anyway?"

"You think it's deep, that's why you can't do it. That's why."

"Who says I can't do it?"

"I know you can't. You haven't."

Well maybe she couldn't and maybe she hadn't. All the people in that world had agreed on a lethal definition of love. It was full of rapture and betrayal and intrigue and she was no good at that. Sydney may belong to this cut-and-thrust world but she didn't. She was not a person who seduced, she found that ultimately unsustainable. Seduction was a sheet of paper folded into secret creases. In these secret creases, Sydney was better.

"So you're saying love is superficial?" She couldn't help herself. She had to bring some snide language into the debate.

Sydney hated that tone in June, that tone after which the only response was to curse. "No. I'm saying it's fucking simple."

"That is not an explanation." June didn't think emotion was ever trustworthy on its own. She preferred reason. Sydney was all impulse, she dismissed June's reason. In fact, Sydney had said as much once. "You have nothing to teach me." June had thought it was emotion speaking and it was, but it was also Sydney, plain and clear.

"Look, do you want to fuck me?"

"Well . . ."

"Do you see what I mean? Simple question, you can't answer."

Where can they go from this question, where? June thinks, as Sydney kisses her, as Sydney touches the place between her breasts and covers June's nipple with her mouth. Where? A short distance, very short. To the bed, or the floor. Half an hour later Sydney seems to think that some depth has been arrived at but June, naked as she might be, feels uncomfortable, restless and unresolved.

"Every second we live," June says, although she is now lying there naked with Sydney again, "every second we live is so commodified we cannot be sure it is the real present."

"What the fuck!" Sydney says, also naked but feeling suddenly clothed. "Why are you saying that now?"

"We cannot be sure there's history, as in events, if each moment is commodified."

There is silence and June thinks that it is the silence occasioned by her profundity. She pauses, letting it sink into Sydney. Then she says, "History, in history things happen, in commodification, things are." Sydney sits up. June notices Sydney's back. Two columns of muscles, a smooth cataract of a backbone, the triangular scapulae and the neck. Is it commodification? No, it is fact, history. The backbone is not a bone per se, it is a tunnel, a long basin. June feels like saying diluvial when she watches Sydney's back, and other words like divulge and gorge. "I don't mean 'are' in the sense of being, but 'are' like never changing, but never giving up anything new."

"Jesus," Sydney says, "Jesus, why?"

June takes this to mean why is commodification unchanging and goes on to explain.

"Well, the thing commodified is supposed to be pleasurable but what is that 'pleasurable'? I mean ... real pleasure changes. It is not the same always, but commodification says it is always the same, which is why people are in the end unhappy because it is in fact the same. It doesn't yield any new sensations ..." Sydney's breasts, for example, are also beautiful and 'beautiful' in this case may be one word but only because of the limitations of a language, not the many ways in which this idea opens up. Sometimes it is the quality of light in the room that makes them so beautiful, other times it is the memory of seeing them in a river, that river in Blue Mountain where they dangerously went naked because whenever June got drunk she became incautious. But nevertheless beautiful is wholly inadequate. Was it the commodification of breasts in general that led to this gaze ... Another part of Sydney, her legs. In snow, Sydney's legs are durable, they look determined as she shovels the walkway. And of course in water they look fractured. Fractured, it is this fracturing that June thinks has ultimately endeared Sydney to her. But Sydney is not fragile in any way. These legs June admires as Sydney rises, these legs are solid. June reaches up to touch them. Sydney says, "I have to go, June."

"You do?"

"Yeah, I really do. Right now. I've had it." Sydney answers, abruptly.

"Ah," June says. It is possible to be in the same place and not the same place, June thinks. She has obviously gone as far as possible with Sydney in this argument. Sydney's left calf has a scar. It's a mark like an interrupted sentence, it fades away and returns near the Achilles. Sydney told June it was from a bicycle spoke. Sydney had stolen a ride on her brother's bicycle and crashed it. See, June thought, even that is beautiful about Sydney's legs, it summons up Sydney flying down a hill on a bicycle.

June is always just about to crack like a thin-shelled egg. Though June thinks her shell is hard, but all shells are fragile even if they're hard. They're shells. She wants Sydney to stay. She won't try to persuade her, though, because then would it be Sydney's desire to stay or June's desire to have Sydney stay? It matters to June. And so in a way, June is for stasis, though of course June thinks of it as the ethics of persuasion. Really June wants Sydney to choose to stay freely. If Sydney can't do that then well, it's fine.

At any rate, just as Sydney's leaving, June says, "Why do you suppose you couldn't do it?"

"Couldn't do what?" Sydney asks.

"The daily embrace and the kindness."

"Fucking Christ, June. We just fucked, didn't we?"

"It's not the same."

"Not the same? Then what is it?"

"It's sex."

"And not the same?"

"No."

Sydney is thrown. All this time Sydney thinks of it as the same. "You got to be kidding me."

"This is the difference between you and me," June says as Sydney drops to the bed. "You think this is the only form of intimacy." Intimacy, intimacy, the word sibilates around the room.

"Okay," Sydney says. "I couldn't do it, all right? I couldn't."

"You are so pessimistic," June says, "Why? Why couldn't you do it?"

"It was too big. It wasn't a small thing at all."

"See," June says.

"You know what, June?"

"What?" June asks.

"You collect sadness."

June is silent. Sydney is silent. The silence reaches the end of the room, the door seems about to close and lock it in. Sydney gets up and opens the door and June thinks Sydney is leaving for sure. But Sydney returns, lies on the bed beside her. And silence hovers and lingers and a little oxygen, which is not the enemy of silence exactly but which can turn silence into its several beings, a little oxygen comes in and makes the silence more variable than it was a minute ago. Because a minute ago the silence was volatile and atomic. June understands the favour Sydney has done her, because June never knows what to do with that kind of silence. It is the silence of endings. So June lies motionless beside Sydney. This quiet is not the same as that silence. It's quiet. The way quiet is sometimes about revelations. Or about something settling.

I suppose I do, June thought. She made a sound but not the sound that came with these words. She didn't want to form any words, she wanted to lie there in quiet.

Sydney put her hand on June's back then and they both said nothing and made no sound and June felt Sydney's hand like a benediction. Yes, June collects sadness. What would happen if no one remembered sadness? We'd walk around mutilated and mutilating and not know how we got there or have any remorse.

"Someone has to," Sydney says, moving her hand up and down June's back. And it was as if Sydney had said the best thing ever to June. June felt Sydney's soothing hand cover her. There is nothing universal or timeless about this love business, Sydney now suspects for the first time. It is hard if you really want to do it right.

ACKNOWLEDGMENTS

Thank you to Louise Dennys most dearly for her rigourous editorial attention; to my patient and critical first readers, Filomena Carvalho, Linda Spalding, Allyson Holder and Madeleine Thien; to my translators and interlocutors, Abdi Osman, Sara Fruner, E.W. and M.O.; and to my agent Sarah Chalfant of the Wylie Agency for her reading and support. A special thanks to Deirdre Molina and Terri Nimmo.

"Love Poem 17" from *The Collected Works* of Xavier Simone is reprinted with permission of the author © Xavier Simone (1968).

DIONNE BRAND's most recent book of poetry is *Ossuaries*, winner of the Griffin Poetry Prize; her nine others include winners of the Governor General's Literary Award, the Trillium Book Award and the Pat Lowther Memorial Award. Her novel *In Another Place, Not Here* was selected as a *New York Times Book Review* Notable Book of the Year and a Best Book by *The Globe and Mail*; *At the Full and Change of the Moon* was also selected as a Best Book by the *LA Times*. Her novel *What We All Long For* was published to great acclaim in Canada, Italy and Germany and won the Toronto Book Award. In 2006, Brand was awarded the Harbourfront Festival Prize for her contribution to the world of books and writing and was Toronto's Poet Laureate from 2009 to 2012. Brand is a professor in the School of English and Theatre Studies at the University of Guelph. She lives in Toronto.